WHAT TO EAT DURING THE APOCALYPSE

VLADIMIR STEFAN

To those who have not given up on a brighter future – may you one day lead the way through your actions and convictions.

First published by Vladimir Stefan, 2024

Copyright © 2024 by Vladimir Stefan

All rights reserved. No part of this publication may be reproduced, stored or transmitted in any form or by any means, electronic, mechanical, photocopying, recording, scanning, or otherwise without written permission from the publisher. It is illegal to copy this book, post it to a website, or distribute it by any other means without permission.

This novel is entirely a work of fiction. The names, characters and incidents portrayed in it are the work of the author's imagination. Any resemblance to actual persons, living or dead, events or localities is entirely coincidental.

Designations used by companies to distinguish their products are often claimed as trademarks. All brand names and product names used in this book and on its cover are trade names, service marks, trademarks and registered trademarks of their respective owners. The publishers and the book are not associated with any product or vendor mentioned in this book. None of the companies referenced within the book have endorsed the book.

First edition

Paperback ISBN: 978-1-0686126-0-2;

E-book ISBN: 978-1-0686126-1-9

Cover art by Christian Storm

Back cover art by Leyla Hunn

INTRODUCTION

Throughout the years, I've had many measures of success – grades, salary, and love life satisfaction. One goal was constant though, and that was writing a book – having a legacy. From the first time I held a book, I felt the power of one. Something that has passed through many hands. To me, it was a symbol of posterity, of leaving something meaningful behind. I was always fascinated and equally pressured by the notion of purpose and have always sought mine. I don't know if this here is the moment I find it, but it has helped to clarify what matters to me and what makes me happy.

Years spent in the corporate environment have made me feel like an empty shell of my former self. I used to write poetry, perform hip-hop, act, and try out new business ideas. Something about being out there always appealed to my sense of freedom – owning myself and my personality. It being squashed under conformity and norms always made for tough, soul-searching moments. And perhaps this moment was my most crucial.

When I sat down to write this for the first time, it was just a funny idea that was worth exploring. I was unemployed and frankly bored and looking for creative ways to fill my time whilst trying to find the perfect next job – as if that exists anymore! An old friend of mine, writing became a solace for the weeks that followed. I have channelled all my inner thoughts and experiences and some of my favourite TV characters and acquaintances to bring Dom and the rest of the story to life.

I purposefully chose the setting for this story to draw attention to the current state of affairs. This is less about a physical apocalypse and more about our internal struggles and collective reactions to the path we have set ourselves upon. I do not want to be preachy or doom-mongering; much of the story is exaggerated or absurdist for the mere point of landing the humour. However, I do hope that my messages, amidst the humour and the pacing of the story, stick - for them to be a moment of reflection and realisation. We are not powerless, and not just individuals – we share this world, this society, and this moment. We have a duty, like others before us, to leave this world a better one for those coming after us. And that is a creed I'll take to the end.

What to Eat During the Apocalypse is about human resilience and laughter in the face of destruction. I have always found humour, and satire in particular, to be a great means of conveying serious messages to the widest of audiences. In Romanian, we have a saying called "a face haz de necaz" which roughly translates as "to laugh at your misfortune" – a universal and uniquely human trait that perhaps has made sure that we haven't faced extinction by our own hands – yet. As such, this book is what you want it to be – a scary story about a realistic future, an absurd satire with elements of dystopia, or a cookbook with too much backstory.

I hope you can laugh, contemplate, and cheer on Dom. He is many of us. Reduced to living day by day, unaware of our powers and our potential. The shackles of routine plaguing our innermost desires to grow and to be authentic may not be broken today, but one day from now. I hope this book brings you as much joy as it brought me to write it – and if it does, I hope you can share it with your world.

Bon appetit.

DAY ZERO

"Get in Mango," I shout across the garden, as the anxious orange cat I've grown to love serves me a hiss and a disapproving look.

"Alright, I'll get the drugs," I say to myself as I move convincingly to grab the bag of catnip from the drawer. This always works – it's got the same effect as a kebab has on British nighttime goers when the lights come on at the end of the night, and they're drawn unconsciously to the meat on the spinning stick like a horde of zombies.

With one shake of the bag, his head is pointing in the right direction and his paws soon follow.

....

Ding-Dong, Ding-Dong

I open the door to be greeted by three voluminous crates and a not-so-voluminous young lad in a dark blue uniform. It's the weekly Christmas of the convenience lover. Long gone are the days of the awkward weekly big shopping trips and the anger-infusing moments queuing up behind that lovely old gran who takes just a bit more time than socially acceptable to sort through her tiny purse to get the exact change.

This is the age of CONTACTLESS! The age of SELF CHECKOUT! And thanks to the pandemic, the normalisation of GROCERY DELIVERIES.

"Tesco order mate. Can I get an autograph?"

"There you go, lad! Long day?" I say awkwardly, knowing the answer is always yes. Even if it is the beginning of the day, the rest of the conversation naturally tends towards negativity and grief. Pure British, that.

I do my little run to the kitchen with the crates and return them gracefully. After all, this is a team effort and we respect hardworking people in this household. Enough to think we are better than them somehow, but not enough to belittle them and not roll up our sleeves. A little nod, a little "Cheers", and we're both on our way. Him to another few hours of breaking his back for the shareholders, and me to cooking myself a scrumptious dinner and watching the latest episode of *Traitors* on the BBC.

With an uncalculated amount of spaghetti thrown in the water, I get the lardons smoking in the pan. I throw a few garlic cloves in too. Why? Well, I do love pissing the Italians off and I do love a bit of garlic. The Parmigiano gets grated and so does the Pecorino in equal parts. Two egg yolks are thrown in, a generous pinch of pepper, and with a masterful whisk, the whole thing comes together. Pasta's *al dente*, the lardons are sizzling – "Alexa, play *That's amore*" – the sounds create an authentically Italian vibe in the heart of Hounslow.

Everything is in sync, life is good. Switch the hob off – spaghetti meets lardons, in with the sauce. Toss. Toss. One more shave of Parmigiano and a dash of pepper and "*que bella*". We've got carbonara - my comfort dish. And two minutes before *The Traitors* starts too – talk about timing.

"*This is the Traitors,*" says Claudia as she's about to take me and a million other people through another day of twists and turns.

The spaghetti hits so well, and often those loose ends splash the corners of the mouth. Nothing a lick can't fix – not the most gracious, but effective nonetheless. Mango is purring and finally finds a spot on the couch after a few rounds of churning "biscuits" on the pillows.

The show pauses and it starts glitching. "Is it the signal?" I wonder. A rainbow-like still image appears on the screen followed by a loud alert sound. A clock starts ticking and the camera pans in on a news presenter.

"Good evening, this is BBC News – we are sorry to interrupt the programme with an emergency transmission."

Oh no, it must be the King. Or maybe it is Adele? Surely not Adele…

"As of ten minutes ago, we have been advised that biological weapons have been deployed against the United Kingdom – we advise you to shelter indoors, covering all ventilation until further…"

And blank. Back to the rainbow and the noise. I look at Mango – he barely flinched a muscle. It's the apocalypse and my cat is sleeping soundly through it.

I stare out the window – I see my neighbours mirroring me in searching the surroundings awkwardly with their gaze, avoiding eye contact as all good

Londoners should do. Nothing seems changed – everything looks fine. Until…

Boom! – one explosion heard far away. It sounded like it was in Acton. Or Soho?

Boom! Boom! – two more explosions. These were closer. But still, no fire can be seen.

The sky is becoming increasingly green-lit. Some jets are flying above. A sort of mist seems to be forming on the street. I see a takeaway delivery rider choking and falling stricken from his moped with food scattering across the road. It looks like sushi. A few people are running scared, choking and holding their chests. Some of them rush to houses at random and start knocking on doors, desperately asking to get in.

Should I maybe go check on the rider? They are paid pretty badly; I wonder if this ordeal will affect his ratings. But ratings aside, what the fuck is actually going on? Why is everyone choking? Am I safe inside?

My neighbours see the scenes and cover their windows. They must've grabbed their kids and started praying to their respective gods. That's what I'd do if I had one, but instead I resort to grabbing Mango and shutting off the TV.

I check my phone. The signal is down and there's no other news. My last notification is Duolingo threatening me to come back to learn French or I'll lose my learning streak.

"*Putain,*" I say to myself. "*C'est la fin du monde.*" And I'll never find out if the *Traitors* stand a chance to win.

. . . .

It's 10 PM and I'm curled up under the duvet. No internet, no signal, no way to distract myself from the existential dread filling me up. "Was it China? Russia? Iran? Did the Americans do one on us? Is it just us? But why Scotland - they're nice and rather progressive up there. Haggis never hurt anyone, bar the sheep and the pigs. Is it the EU in response to Brexit?"

The bed feels incredibly small now. The green light fills up the sky and radiates into the room. I feel like a sex worker in Amsterdam, but my boss is Shrek. It's all so quiet. All you can hear are occasional screams in the distance fading away. Are they existential screams or orgasms? To be fair, there's no better time to squeeze one in. Grab your loved one, have some raucous sex, try something new, maybe invite that flatmate that you always thought could join in but you didn't want to ruin the atmosphere at games night. Your relationship is doomed, but apparently so is the rest of the world, so why not have at it one more time – might be the last.

"Would it be appropriate to rub one out?" People talk about post-nut clarity and sadness but I'm wondering if this time it will have the opposite effect. Will it be the seed of *hope*? The all-tension releaser? But there's no porn – fuck. I guess I could just let my imagination run amok. Just like the olden days. As I close my eyes, however, another jet flies past, rendering my efforts useless and reminding me of the situation. Frustrated, I give up and begrudgingly cover myself in shame.

Ok, let's try doing something productive. If there's anything the sad corporate life taught me, it's that every danger can be turned into an opportunity. It's time to assess the situation and bring out the post-it notes. Big questions to ask:

What do I know so far? What resources do I have available and how long will they last? How can I communicate or receive communications?

Good, that's done now.

However, I never learned how to deal with these types of questions myself. I'm much better at asking them and then getting a huddle or some juniors to brainstorm some ideas. And then collect the glory by presenting their work as mine. Just your usual corporate food chain where I used to eat very well.

Could this mean the end of corporations? No more 9-5s and the dreadful commute? Are we finally going to become an agrarian society, organised around a commune? *The Commune of Hounslow*. Where the co-op is a way of life and not a more expensive type of Tesco. Trading sugar for honey, fruit for veg, instant coffee for oat milk (duh, no more cows!). No division amongst Tories or Labour, north or south, brexiteers or remainers, British or immigrants, and more importantly none of these MBGA arseholes. Just people living in harmony and for the common good…

Boom! Boom! Two more pounds interrupt my socialist utopia. Some sirens can be heard in the distance. I rise on the bed and peek through my roof windows – there are some lasers pointed towards the sky, rising from various areas in the distance. Usually, that would mean some concert or big event, but this time – what do they mean?

"Big lights through the sky."

"What?" I reply.

Was that a voice I heard, or did I just have my first auditory hallucination? It could be stress-induced, but weirdly I feel no stress. Just confusion and a lack of control. And for some reason, a sense of calm and tranquillity, likely due to spending two years cooped up during the pandemic.

I did have her with me back then, though. Ah, she was gorgeous and kind, with a smile that could light up the room and that would've pierced through these green-lit skies. Why green though? It's oddly a trope, isn't it? Like "golden hour" filters in movies when the action is set in Mexico. If I am to live, as suggested, through an apocalypse, I do wish for it to be slightly more novel – a pink one, maybe? Or purple, even. Show me the end of the world in a gradient purple.

Ok, focus. Meditate, control your breathing, and start: **What do I know so far?** Well, we've been told to stay indoors and that there are biological weapons. The sky is green and the air makes people cough now. The delivery driver fell from his moped. *"Is he still there?"* I check – he is. The neighbours seem fine, in their homes, although I couldn't know for sure. The air may not filter in, oddly. Inside seems safe.

What resources do I have available and how long will they last? I've done my weekly shop which will likely last me a week. Plus, all the pantry stuff that I meticulously bought for when inevitable poverty catches us all. We all need rice, pasta, and some tins of protein, as a minimum. I did also stock up on Mango's food so there's that if this goes on for longer... *but no*, not at his expense.

Although, will I have to rethink my love for him if shit hits the fan and my stomach starts grumbling? Maybe I'll do what they did in the Andes back in the 70s when that plane crashed. I'm pretty sure if I check-out before he does, he will not hesitate to treat himself to a good portion of human steak. And come to think of it, the opportunity would be immensely in his favour – I could last him a good month or so, that's even before he gets to the bones. What can he give to me, though? A few meals? Not to mention the emotional toll and impact that eating him will have on me. But I digress...

Back to resources. I'm okay in this department, they will last a week or more, although a lot of my food is perishable so I'd have to make good use of it and prioritise as much as I can. Can't risk foodborne illnesses during biological warfare - that's like having a heart attack during a funeral: bad timing, bigger picture going on.

How can I communicate with others? There should be some ways I could reach others. Radio could work? I've seen enough "end-of-the-world" flicks to know that the smart guys always search for a radio first. But then again, I come from a generation born with Google, and one thing I didn't ever google was "How do you use radios as a means of communication?" Thankfully, I did search once "Why is my poop green?" and the answer to that may mean nothing today. But why is the sky green definitely would be of interest – it really does baffle me.

Maybe I can devise some code? Something to help me contact others, like an Ouija board but for the living. Yeah, I can stick it in the window, and hopefully inspire others to do the same, that should open some dialogue. I remember the days of having to press the phone digits 100 times to convey a two-sentence text message. But these young ones may not connect with that. Forget them, they need to catch up this time and feel left behind. Like a lost traveller in the deep Amazonian Forest, I will seek the oldest of the household to communicate with - the "elder" of the tribe. My peer.

. . . .

It's 2 AM. I haven't heard any more explosions or jets flying; the silence is ghostly. I'm exhausted and my eyes feel dry and heavy. Maybe a shuteye won't hurt. I've got to conserve energy and be ready for whatever challenge tomorrow may bring. Will I be able to sleep, I wonder? Normally at this point, I'd ask Alexa to play me some rain sounds to help me relax and ease into whatever crazy dream sequence my subconscious plans for me. But there's no Alexa, no music platforms, no porn, and the darkness of the room is tainted by the green light cracking through the window curtains. That green fucking sky, what's up with that?

DAY ONE

The light feels like a welcome gift. I woke up feeling weird, as if I just came back to life from a bad dream. For only a brief second, I thought that last night's events were just a figment of my imagination and today will be a bright new day where I put on my trousers and head to the café down the road, carefully ignoring all needs for social interaction. Ah, a flat white right now would mean the world!

But there are no flat whites anymore. Our bohemian ways are now gone. It's the dawn of a new humanity, where only the strong and isolated shall make it through. Do we even have a government anymore? The army was prepared, hence the jets? Or was it the enemy scouting the damage?

Mango is sitting on top of my chest in a display of

dominance. Or threat? Maybe he heard my inner thoughts last night and decided to remind me that at no point is he afraid to survive, starting with my face. I grab him gently, yet overpoweringly, to remind him as well that whilst I'm here, I am very capable of man-handling him. Feeling heavy, I push myself against the bed and seem to find the power to get up and draw the window curtains.

The mist is still present and now has a weird beige tint to it. "Beige" or creamy yellow? Never got colours, as, after all, I am a simple man. I know five colours and different levels of describing intensity, that's it.

It used to piss her off. It's funny how simple elements of communication make up for disagreements. Was it ignorant on my behalf, or a bit too much for her to expect that a guy must know the whole Pantone range of colours? How is that helping us now, Yasmin? The mist is now fucking Pantone 6345#, *baby piss yellow faded*. Good luck with that information!

That small win of the argument in my head provides a short-lived grin. "Oh my god! BIRDS!" I think as I see some small objects flying in the distance. Can't tell if they're flapping wings or not. Something is flying and it's not a jet! I wonder if those guys who believed that birds are a government conspiracy are seeing this. Thousands of years of evolution and social contracts and the guys that think birds are robots sent to spy on us win. A bit bittersweet that sometimes I wish to have my intelligence insulted and proven wrong. There's something quite grounding about that – reminding yourself that you're not as smart as you think and ultimately you are still someone's nutjob sometime, somewhere.

I head down the stairs and it all feels normal. The weight of my feet, the creaking of wood, the smell of worn-down carpet and clothes drying up. For some reason, it seems that electricity and gas are still working. Imagine the bills after this is all over with everyone stuck indoors. I'm grateful for power in the face of Armageddon but I'm scared of British Power and the current tariff I'm on.

"The kettle!" The staple of British existence. There would be anarchy without a cuppa during the apocalypse; we would collapse in a collective suicidal action before the Chinese get to us. Or maybe Iran? Is the commonwealth finally fighting back???

I let the water boil and luckily, I've been blessed with 80 bags of fine English tea from last night's shopping.

One sugar and one milk - described as a one second flick of the wrist with the carton, enough to splash, not enough to overpower. A quick smell, a quick sip, an "*ahh*!" and a quick stare down the garden.

The trees have lost their leaves, and the grass's green colour has vanished – it looks like a monotone, melancholic painting. That's why they call it biological warfare – it goes after biology first. This makes for a perfect depressing pop album cover.

The sound of music! Ah! Didn't realise I missed it so much. Luckily, I've downloaded a few songs in my lifetime, so I can at least have some background music whilst I contemplate the inevitability of death, and whether I can overpower a militia with a butter knife and a rolling pin. The perfect dream hero scenario, where I ultimately save the day despite the odds stacked infinitely against me.

My downloaded playlist is a weird one thanks to her – she wanted to add some songs of her own for when we were driving through the countryside with no signal. I'm now stuck with odd choices. It's between Cardi B, Tupac, Taylor Swift, the Rolling Stones, Vivaldi and a podcast on the woman's menstrual cycle and its effects on energy throughout the day. If I die and my playlist lives, it will tell whatever civilisation finds us about our culture. The multidimensional experience of life, the sadness, the joys, the *WAP*. We had it all and we gave it away for conflict. I bet the Greeks or the Mayans predicted this. That we'll achieve so much and navigate the world of diplomacy and international relations, only to be bludgeoned by the most common element of humanity: destruction.

I open the fridge as hunger is creeping in. I grab a few eggs, some cheese, and an abandoned piece of ham from the deeper end of the fridge. The first 8 pieces of the pack of ham were gracefully used for sandwiches, all having a role in a symbiotic pairing with bread, and then there's *him*. Ripped to pieces by overly keen fingers trying to separate the slices, to be only used as an undesired ingredient in a mix of leftovers to provide sustenance.

I crack the eggs, which makes me realise that whilst we have not answered the age-old question of which was first, we do know for sure which will be last. The eggs will be last. I beat them up with a pinch of salt and throw them in the pan. With careful circular motions, I make sure to allow for the eggs to meet the whole of the pan. Add some cheese, some pieces of ham in and then start rolling it up. Pick it up and serve it in a dish with some toast ... and then it hit me.

As I was narrating all of this in my head, I realised what I needed to do. To keep my sanity and to keep occupied until God knows when, I shall write a cookbook! One where I just make use of whatever supplies I have left, thanks to my last shopping delivery: **What to Eat During the Apocalypse.** I may never get to publish it, and I might die before I write my first recipe, but what a way to depart with a gift to humanity or whatever civilisation finds us next.

So, it was all set. This will be my apocalyptic hobby. "It's good for your mental health to have hobbies," my therapist used to say. I never had many when life was good, but somehow, whilst staring death in the eyes, I find the power to try something new! Maybe that's just how I work – positive reinforcements bring no effect. I need the threat of existence, or lack of it, to get me moving. If I ever get out of this, I'm going to paint, with all five colours in different shades of intensity. And I'll ask my therapist to slap me with the paintbrushes until marks start showing on my wrists as a reminder that there is no pleasure without pain.

Bleak thoughts of life through the apocalypse start to stress me out. I go to check my TV to see if I had any movies or shows downloaded previously and to my luck, there are two seasons of The Office US. Funnily enough, this was also my pandemic show. Something about this show brings comfort through the worst of times.

It might be the simplicity and naturality of it all. We were all just basic workers, going about our day-to-day lives, forced together socially by the workplace. People who would naturally not develop any relationship were suddenly expected to spend eight hours in each other's company, oversharing, overstepping and overcompensating. On top of it all, overworking for no other reason than keeping a roof above our heads. All trying to fit in through what is expected of us. What a crazy social experiment.

And to think that, back in the day, that's how most relationships were formed. And my generation did the swipe. Later we found out that one *swipey* app was not enough - we had to have many more. *Let our algorithms pair you up, you horny, lonely and lovely paying customers. Let us tell you how worthy you are(n't).*

Well, how worthy are we now though? All past and working social norms have been discarded. I used to think unjustifiably highly of myself as an account manager at a bank. As if money was my value and my social status was dictated by the suit I was wearing.

And here we are. Pretty sure I'm bottom of the pecking order now. Who needs someone with customer service or stakeholder management experience now? Someone who can upsell customers or handle complaints? There are no shareholders to bring value for now. No customers to satisfy and no stock price to increase. The firemen, doctors and soldiers must be in high demand right now. Bet you'd want one of those to help you with survival. Those guys and girls have skills that can be used in a situation like this. The most I can do is a PowerPoint on why the apocalypse could turn out to be an investment opportunity and recommend some changes to the occupying management.

The beauty of capitalism failing is that it shows us exactly why our moral praise system is fucked up. It flips it over and we now realise that at a basic human level, when capital and profit are discarded, certain skills sit at the top of the pyramid, and former gourmands are now bottom feeders.

I can't watch *The Office* now. I need to make myself useful and get a sense of purpose instead of just waiting to be saved like a *prima donna*. There's no charming prince to save me, and even if there is he's probably coughed his lungs out already from that toxic gas that the Saudis (or the Indians?) dropped on us. Probably best to pick my washing up before it gets mouldy. You have to have fresh clothes if you're taken prisoner.

There are a few things I still care about and weirdly enough, right now, appearance seems to be one of them. Decades of marketing have convinced me, even in the event of an apocalypse, that it's not what you are but how you look that matters to others. If I were to be captured by occupation forces seeking account managers for whatever society they have ready for us, I need to dress the part for the role.

I pick the clothes one by one, starting from the top with the heavy load. Which reminds me, I used to have a flatmate that would do their clothes drying all wrong. There is such a thing – I'm adamant that you go from heavy to light, top-down, not the other way around. Colours don't matter, I'm not a psychopath. Now, this agent of chaos would have her knickers and socks at the top and hoodies at the bottom on the rack. I may be wrong, but I thought we all agreed on this, a long time ago, and that was just weird to see.

There are two things I can think of that work heavy at the bottom and light at the top, and that is pears and Christmas trees. And slight variations of vegetation. It just irked me to the point I wanted to rearrange her laundry or take them off and leave them on the floor. Kind of like ruining a puzzle in a fit of rage. I hope she is well enough through this though, and in these dire times, decided to join the rest of society on mutually agreed terms.

....

"Meow Meow, Bitch."

Mango greets me with a lick on his lips. Do cats have lips? Or just gums. I swear I heard him say "Bitch." I wouldn't be surprised, given his attitude in general. I'd imagine at the very least I'd get a capital "B" with the slur, as a little token of appreciation. When did we agree as humans, in this world of dogs, panda bears, and cute piglets, to choose the one species that actively shows their indifference to us as our favourite companion? Or worthy of the same praise as dogs and their unwavering loyalty? Honestly, big thanks to our palaeolithic ancestors for braving up to pet the wolves, you did us a solid one.

It's the "purr". It must possess hypnotic properties because it genuinely softens us up. It's 2 PM and he's hungry now, understandably. One pouch of the 4% derivative meat and he's in it. Poor Mango, a victim of consumerism. He's addicted to these pouches that have basically no nutritional value. If I gave him shrimp, chicken, or any other meats that his ancestors would rip my hand up for, he would just ignore it. He will not eat anything but jelly-stocked pieces of unidentifiable meat.

If I go first and he does not eat me, he would deserve it. He has lost the most innate survival skills that made his species continue through millennia. Like humans being gluten-free and allergic, unlucky drawers of the genetics lottery, handpicked to fear death by almonds or corn, so too will he be dead by years of meat pouch addiction and a lack of conservation in the face of starvation. The prick will show his indifference to me even as I lay there with 85 kilograms of good protein.

Upon feeding the four-legged lodger, I decide to prep myself something too, writing notes in my book as I go along. A tin of cannellini beans dried up and then mixed in some stock, spices, and some sausages that I'm frying in the pan. Vegetarian sausages this time – I said I'd cut down on meat and here I am eating a mush of peas and 150 other ingredients and stabilisers to do my part in saving the world that's dying currently, whilst Taylor Swift is using a private jet to get her groceries. Could kill for a Cumberland sausage now and climate change could not care a bit. In fact, I'm pretty sure that is ranking low on the agenda now given that the air seems to kill, and we were already on a path of rushing to climate change.

Anyway, everything's on the plate, with some boiled carrots to the side. Easy lunch. I end up playing some *Office* for background noise because I am a millennial who has been brought up with TV as a distraction, and deep introspection while chewing gives me anxiety. With all of that done, I need to focus on the next productive task. I need to be a valuable member of society now.

I remember that last night I was thinking of drawing a Ouija board as a way of communicating with the outside. I don't know why I thought of this first; perhaps years of climate change guilt have made me consider the most reusable options. So, I sit down at my desk and bring an A3 sheet in front of me. The desk –

my work-from-home set-up – is now a remnant of a life of work that surely is behind me. *The Commune of Hounslow* is a brighter future, one where I shall grow potatoes for the greater good and where we regulate our communal needs through barter and individual contributions to the betterment of our society.

I start drawing up. I need "yes" and "no" answers there. This is England so I must add a "Sorry" there too. We love saying sorry for everything, no biological weapon could stop that. Apologising is key to British survival. Now, I have a laser, so my thinking here is this. Place the paper up on the windows and from behind, use a laser pointer to circle out the various letters as they follow. May not allow for long narratives, or the traditional small chat, but should hopefully allow us to exchange some words.

I go to the window and start placing it up. The two neighbours to my left have boarded their house up. The one in front seems to just have their curtains drawn and the other one to my right, in classical British fashion, exhibits their whole indoors through the big windows to the lounge. Two kids are playing Monopoly there, what a time to do so. Land on Chance and oh no, *'you've encountered Biological Armageddon – society collapses. Go purge your neighbours' houses and never go to jail because it doesn't exist anymore."*

The innocence of learning Monopoly as a kid, bonding with your friends – the same friends you want to kick out of the house, years later, when you land at their hotel in Mayfair, and they rip the skin off you in rent payments. There will be no Monopoly in the Commune, it will only be the Cooperative. No one wins, but no one loses either, and we all play the game with an equal chance. There are only Community Chests, and everyone has a go at it. No land is more valuable than others, they all serve a unique purpose.

Haven't thought yet about how you'd win, so I guess it does sound slightly boring, but in the future, boring will be sought after. Mundane will be appreciated. The lack of hustle and competition will be replaced by cooperation and enlightenment. And with any luck, communal brunches.

....

She was touching my hand, acting shy, telling me "We should go in". Another party where I get to meet another round of her friends. How many friends does this woman have or need? My cut-off is in single digits.

I just find it overwhelming to maintain similar levels of engagement or time with that many people.

Plus, do you really like them all? Or do you just like what they represent at certain times? I have a hilarious friend, Mike who always pops a joke, mostly inappropriate but never offensive. I would love to have him mingle with others, but I always feel like I'd be walking on eggshells.

The trickiest part of our current culture is the multifaceted complexity of one's feelings and experiences. We're not all cut of the same cloth and oftentimes that can make for muddy waters. What's a joke to someone can evocate strong traumas for others. People always tell you to "be yourself" but often enough, that comes with many risks trying to fit in, making it a game. Try a few things, read the room, and decide on which personality to deploy today. *Be one version of yourself* much rather, play it safe.

"Are you coming?" says Yasmin, with some warm eyes, as if she's rescuing a puppy left on the side of the road, rain pouring all over him.

"That's what she said!" I attempt a joke, but it does not get more than a supportive giggle. "Yes. Fine. But if that boring lesbian couple is there, we are not listening to another house issue story. Please."

She nodded in agreement. I should clarify at this point that I always found queer people very engaging and energetic. Until I got stuck with Yasmin at an after-party in our early days of dating. We were in this room surrounded by very high people and to our left was a couple, inconspicuous looking, that Yasmin started talking to.

These girls had just moved in and were describing their house. Through a very unexplainable twist of events, or the effects of the cocaine, one of the girls went to lengths describing the number of light switches in the property. This demon with girlish features had spent minutes on end describing the placement, counting the numbers, and making the case for more, or less, light switches. If Nikola Tesla would've heard this story, he would've been *shocked*.

Through a vocal enough look at my future girlfriend, I made it clear that one more light switch story and I shall seek the first window to throw myself out from, leaving myself at the mercy of the softness of what I land on.

Fortunately, that lesbian couple weren't in this time. Just the cool gays and a few straights. I can deal with this. We start dancing and the light is gorgeously reflected on her face. I might be in love, I thought to myself at that time. It all just seemed right. I lean over to kiss her, and we get lost in the moment.

......

With a gasp of air, I woke up. An erection has found its way into this anticlimactic environment. The world was burning outside yet I was nostalgic horny, the worst type. Most of the horny states find themselves in the present or future made-up scenarios, but here I was turning up for past events. Some weird form of past-tense sexual desire, or PTSD. But I guess that's how the horny mind works when there is no future, and the present is uncertain: we glorify the past. We yearn for it.

The recipe for my penis activating right now is the same recipe for racism and nationalism. And truth is, despite all the good, sexually appealing, companionship moments – we were not right for each other. Not on that deeper level, future-proof, values-aligned shared belief system. I was running in the rat race, and she wanted to walk, to enjoy the journey. I wanted the destination, destroying everything in my path for my linear vision of what the future should be and how success is measured. Rushing up the future, so I can eventually relax and take a breath. Admit that I've finally made it.

And here I am drawing Ouija boards to communicate with my neighbours because Angola or Lithuania decided to erase London. I go upstairs to see if my neighbours picked up on my intention. The ones to the right decided to put cardboard crosses on their windows and scribe "Satan will not win!" Do these guys think I'm trying to conjure the dead here? I see one of the kids staring through the window. I put my laser pointer up and highlight the letters **R U O K.** The kid turns around and a long motherly arm drags him from the window and into the abyss of the living room. The same mother returns, closing the curtains and daggering me with her eyes.

The dawn is nearing its completion, and a few jets fly past. By now, I've got used to the sound of jets crossing the sky. A sky which remains green, and I'm starting to enjoy this vibe. There is something quite ubiquitous about what I'm experiencing now, so for a second I stop, contemplating it deeply. The night used to be so dark and boring and now it feels like the sky is the ceiling at a reggae venue. Bob Marley's

"One Love" starts playing in my head. Some tingles of hope are felt on my spine.

It's dinner time and both me and Mango are roaming around the kitchen in disbelief. He's licking his manhood while staring me down in a twisted contest of who *chickens* out and gets uncomfortable first – and it's always me. Always gets me thinking about the norms of our society where you can't just get a moment to yourself to groom, irrespective of place. Some partners have allowed us the occasional rearrangement of the crown jewels within the comfort of our homes, but for most part, that is frowned upon. An uncomfortable feeling, followed by an unstoppable urge, limited by rules imposed through decency decrees. The freedom of the animal is very appealing to the common man. We dread their dependency but salute their shameless decision-making.

"Anyway, what was up with my neighbours?" I think to myself as I transfer a cod fillet into the oven. Some potatoes are sent to roast on their own and I'm putting together some onion, garlic and basil to bathe in olive oil on a high heat. When the fish and the potatoes are done, I'll top it with the magic oil. "I get they're scared but Satan is a bit of a stretch. Have they gone mad maybe?" I wouldn't put it past them. We never exchanged any words previously and I'm pretty sure they never had a chance to form an opinion of me. And I'm sure I'm not helping my case right now.

The power suddenly goes down. The smoke alarm starts chirping. The irony of the death-inducing gas outside of my front door and my smoke alarm protecting me from $CO2$, but anyway, *whadafuc*. I was cool with the end-of-the-world scenario as long as I had some palliative care in the form of electricity to get me through. Just enough so I can run a few meals before resorting to eating out of tins. I'm now at the mercy of the MBGA government. Or our Turkish overlords. Bulgarian, maybe?

The fish is luckily done so I light one of the many candles that she got for us. I never understood women's fascination with candles but I was not one to judge, as I had my weird fascinations that did not make sense to her. I was obsessed with collecting car models, for example. She called them *toys*, the simpleton. I miss those teasing fights whilst I'm having a lonesome candlelit dinner with a *bacalao a lagareiro*. That's the name of the Iberian recipe. If the Portuguese come through the door right now to take me as a prisoner, I might be lucky and get sent to a nice sandy, beach-side prison.

It's time to sacrifice one beer from the fridge. I've been trying to cut down on alcohol recently, and I now realise this is the worst of times to cut down. So I find myself with only a 4-pack of weak lager to ration over however long this will take. I get small sips in between bites of fish and spud and stare at the wall. It's just the end of the first day since the events of last night and I'm feeling like I will lose my mind by the dawn of tomorrow, if I even get to see it until the end.

I go to the sofa and stare out of the window at the green sky. No jets have been flying for the past four hours. I wonder if whatever has happened might've made the Aurora Borealis visible from Hounslow. I can't see any stars past this smoky green blanket.

Mango joins me on the sofa and resumes his groin care.

"You don't know anything about all this, do you?"

Stares at me. Meows.

"It's just you and me now buddy. Want some fish?"

Smells the fish, turns his head, and returns to his groin. I lay my head on the cushion and finally manage to shut my eyes.

......

I'm running on a hill backwards. Why am I running backwards?

A star shoots down. An unknown evil face with a long moustache, someone looking like a cross between the Monopoly guy and Colonel Sanders, comes towards me. Is that why I'm going backwards? Need to check where I'm heading. Without realising I was heading towards a cliff. I fall and twist and turn comically as I'm going down fast to the undeniably painful stop at the bottom of this hole. One hand reaches and stops me. It's Yasmin. She pulls me into a cave. What a strong woman. I dust myself off and proceed to hug her. The cave is dimly lit by three massive candle jars.

We sit down and I tell her about the evil man with the long moustache. She looks like she pretends to listen to me but she seems uninterested, although also relieved to have me there in one piece. She lunges towards me and starts kissing my neck, telling me it's alright now and that she will protect me. The atmosphere goes from thriller to erotic, in classical fashion.

I feel slightly emasculated to have been rescued by her, but realise that this is just my toxic masculinity showing off and I was just minutes ago pissing myself running away from Colonel Sanders. I reciprocate the kiss and all of a sudden, I'm teleported to Mexico and it's the golden hour, just like in those Hollywood movies. Antonio Banderas awaits by a yellow taxi with a Cuban cigar in his mouth. He opens the door and tells me we have business to do. The people need me.

....

"Meow-Meow. Bitch. Get up."

I wake up shocked and with a weird sense of duty towards the people. Was it the Mexicans? Mango stares me down, sitting on top of my chest again, with his face an inch closer to mine than last time. I don't know if I can go back to sleep now. I'm starting to feel paranoid that he might actually eat me. What if he does understand the complexity of the situation and grooming his groin is just a coping mechanism? Or maybe it's his *antipasti* before the mains. He finds a spot and curls up by my arm. For once in the past 30 hours, I feel like he knows I'm a bit scared. We're just two scared boys who've only got each other.

YEARS BEFORE

I didn't know what to think of her at the beginning. She was a very warm and calming presence, but I was used to chaos. I thought our ways of life would end up being destructive to each other. She was a dreamer and I thought I was a realist. I was living here, in the real world where money dictates everything – from comfort to aspirations. She was just comfortable getting by and taking life one day at a time. I thought she was naïve, but at the same time, her ambition inspired me. With time, I grew to love all her quirks and outlooks. And now I watch her getting ready as we're about to go for our anniversary dinner, where I will propose to her.

"What?" she asks, catching my adoring glance.

"I just think you are gorgeous and I'm one lucky guy."

"I am and you are, indeed. Okay, I'm done in a second. Have you fed Mango?"

Shit. Mango. "I think he's outside, I'll call him in."

The suit trousers are strangling my crotch as I'm going down the stairs, making every move a struggle to control letting out a high-pitch squeal. The last few months of indulging in takeaways have left a mark. If the apocalypse comes and flesh-eating zombies start chasing us down the street, I might have to save Yasmin by offering myself. A sprint right now looks highly improbable without the realistic risk of tearing my scrotum.

"Get in, Mango!"

I shout as he joyously taps his paws on the grass and joins us inside. I feed him his favourite pouch of food and proceed to put my jacket on. I carefully place the ring box inside the jacket and make my way outside. Yasmin joins me, grabs my arm, and we start heading to the tube.

The loud Piccadilly line train transitions through the West of London taking us into the heart of the West End. She is resting her head on my shoulder and we people watch, occasionally whispering to each other makeshift stories of those people.

"See that guy there with the blue hat? How much do you want to bet that his wife picked that hat for him?"

"How do you know it's a miss? Could be a dude." I tell her, feeling proud of myself as I have won the games of diversity and inclusivity. "Bit reductionist of you to think that way. I bet when I say doctor you imagine a guy too. Check your unconscious bias, miss."

She slaps my shoulder, lovingly but defeated. She is such an open-minded character that it brings me so much pleasure to tease her on every occasion when she is not being ultra-inclusive or careful with her words.

"The next stop is Leicester Square. Please mind the gap."

"...Between rich and poor!" she interjects with an adorable grin on her face. I smile back and chuckle.

We walk up the stairs and head into the bustling street. There must be tens of thousands of people right here in the same GPS coordinates. London is so overwhelming sometimes. We always thought we should move out. She was ready anytime, but I wasn't. The corporate ladder had a few more steps and I was ready to take them.

She wanted a little countryside cottage and jokingly said we could establish our commune there and live off only farm produce and self-sustain. The idiot. We would be so bored. We needed the bustling city. Of course, I didn't tell her that and I just made up excuses to delay. Her supporting nature accepted them, and she didn't want me to resent her for moving away, giving up on my prospects and self-made wet dreams of success.

The cloudy sky became more menacing and started raining upon us in a flash and, without a change in pace or demeanour, the Londoners around us opened their brollies, and so did we, in a synchronised understanding of the situation. The tourists went hiding in stores, putting bags above their heads and taking photos or videos of the city under the shower. Now they can tell their friends they experienced the classic London rain.

I rush Yasmin to the theatre; we get the tickets and go inside. Quick shake of the brolly and we are sat down ready to watch this show called *The Vagina Monologues*. Oh yeah, she was a feminist too. I guess I am one as well, but due to the male circles I've been in, I have always felt a bit awkward using the label, though I do agree with the politics of it all.

She loves listening to podcasts and exploring her understanding of the struggles of women both in the West and further out. A few times she has opened my eyes to issues I was blissfully, or by choice, ignorant to. I always respected and admired her dedication to class struggles, despite at times not agreeing with her viewpoints. Her intelligence and curiosity were traits I admired at length, in contrast to her utopic dreams of communes and self-sustaining life. Real-world problems can have real solutions – *not everything is anarchy, set the parliament on fire, have a tea, and it will all be fine.*

The show draws to its inevitable conclusion:

"Did you enjoy that?" she asks, as we are getting up and ready to leave.

"Yeah – it was alright. You owe me watching football this weekend."

"Who've we got?"

"Villa away. Going to be a big one."

As I mention football, two vividly emotional ladies give me a death stare, as I have violated the sanctity of the safe space by mentioning the grotesque spectacle of kicking balls with one's feet. The epitome of toxic masculinity to some feminists. Not to my Yasmin. She's a converted Geordie, *black and white soldier.*

"Aye, they don't stand a chance with our current run of form," she says, while glaring over to the two ladies as if she was trying to protect me. My lady just swung her massive penis in front of these ladies. I'm in love.

The restaurant is a 15-minute walk away and the rain has intensified. I offer her my coat as the temperature has dropped and one of this lovely woman's flaws is to never dress appropriately for all stages of the night. What's good for 5 PM is not good for 8 PM on a March evening. It's too early to be that much of a believer.

We arrive at Cucina, her favourite Italian restaurant, and we are greeted with champagne by the owner, whom we've gotten to know over time. He is celebrating three years in business and two and a half years of us as his favourite patrons, we like to think.

We sit down and she orders from the vegetarian menu - she has progressively switched to the leafy side of dieting, leaving me to tend to my cravings for meat dishes. I tell her that if we do get a farm, I am not giving up on meat, that's one of my conditions.

I will not just grow potatoes and carrots and have nut roast for dinner. I am willing to change my ways gradually, but too much of a shock to the system can harm, and I'm nowhere near that strong.

"I will have the carbonara please."

"And I will have the courgette pasta."

"Did you know that courgettes were once a remedy for Mad Cow Disease?" That was me – I was a fun facts guy.

"Ah really, how come?"

"They squashed the beef!"

She's unimpressed. Back at home, she would give me a big laugh, but in high society, she would rather not encourage this behaviour. I always had this thing for using humour to get people's validation. That's how I caught her, too. Making bad puns confidently. I smile proudly and when the waiter brings the food, I repeat the joke.

He doesn't understand. He's Italian. I had to repeat Mad Cow Disease twice and got looks from tables next to us. Yasmin was slightly embarrassed but tried to hide it. She is resilient, this one.

I avoid further humiliation by trying to maintain a romantic atmosphere for the rest of the dinner. After all, I can be Brad Pitt charming too, not just silly Ryan Reynolds kind of charming. We eat, we laugh, and we talk about our adventures over the past years. The good, the bad, the ups and downs. I run her through all my appreciative thoughts of her and she reciprocates as the momentum is building up. I see the owner bringing another bottle of champagne towards our table. I lean over to kiss her; I tell her how much she means to me and I get down on one knee, by her side.

DAY TWO

I wake up to the smell of smoke. I get up in a rush to check the whole house. It all seems fine inside. I check out the window and one of the boarded houses to my left is on fire. Were they inside? I want to check and see if I can help but that gas outside seems dangerous. The takeaway rider's body is still out there, as a stark reminder of how perilous this situation is.

I try shooting some lasers inside the house to draw their attention with no luck. I check my phone again, still no signal, and even then, do we still have firemen? There were no screams for help, or none that I could hear. Maybe they were never home. But who boarded the windows from the inside?

I see my neighbour in front checking, scared, through his window to see if the fire is reaching their house. They catch a glimpse of me! I wave and point to the Ouija board.

R U O K

The guy waves back with one thumb up. I point with the laser again and circle the whole board.

DO 1 U 2

The lad gives me a thumbs-up again and disappears into his house. I keep an eye on the fire which seems to slowly be extinguishing without moving to the next house. The mist outside seems even more faded. I'm wondering if the gases are rising up and if soon enough it will be safe to go outside. There's been no sign of the authorities yet. No indication of what it could be or how we can get through this.

Tired of waiting for the guy to come back, I glance around the neighbourhood. The family to my right is in the living room standing in a circle with something in the middle of them. They bow down simultaneously and rise, singing praise to the sky, or the chandelier at the very least. I wondered if they have resorted to cultish ways and are performing a sacrifice now.

They run around that inanimate object, which I cannot tell for the life of me what it is, in some sort of ritualistic dance. One of the kids seems off, like not wanting to be part of it. The mother spots me and makes everyone stop. Flips me the middle finger and then shuts the blinds again. Well, at least they are okay.

I wonder if in the Commune we will have religion. Before all this, Islam took a massive lead over Christianity in the religious championships. Christians did well for some centuries and then the ultimate secularisation of the West tamed some of those ambitions. Maybe new religions will arise after this. I'm pretty sure there will be no shortage of prophets going on TikTok, and getting a following. Maybe it will be the Bird people. Flipping us all off with the smug "I told you so" that conspiracists never get a chance to say. Birdhism? Birdianity? The chaos should eventually tone down and people will find communion once again. And who's to say we can't all venerate the pigeons? Once the rats of the skies, now the rulers of the world. A true *rats-to-riches* story.

My neighbour returns to the window with a big whiteboard.

"Aw, the fucker," I think to myself. He is singlehandedly saving civilisation with his whiteboard and here I am with my Ouija board looking like a sad, death-conjuring nerd. The post-apocalyptic glory goes to Gerrard, who is about to give me a masterclass in sustainable communication.

IS IT JUST YOU THERE?

Don't understand the point of the question as he's not about to barge in and save me from loneliness. But I respond using the **Yes**.

A sense of guilt grows inside me. I know Mango is here too, but I forgot about him for a brief second. And in all movies, it's women and children first, men if they're lucky. Never pets. I raise my hand at Gerrard in a *"wait!"* move. I grab Mango from downstairs and raise him by the window, conveying that it's me and him.

Gerrard nods and disappears from the window.

Now I'm left standing there stuck with Mango, staring at the window while Gerrard runs away with the information that it's just me and my cat.

I drop Mango down a bit too violently for his liking.

"Meow-Meow. Fuck you. Bitch. Meow."

Gerrard returns with his own cat and grins like an idiot.

L O L I laser on my Ouija. He then disappears casually as if we're just two socially awkward introverts running into each other on a busy high street.

Not wanting to look too desperate, I accept the nature of our small talk and head to the kitchen to make some brunch. I grab some spinach and eggs and a couple of slices of bread. Going to make myself a nice egg Florentine and write down the recipe for future generations that will come across my book. "Spinach goes wrong fast, especially in an apocalypse, so always make good use of it."

I wonder if Jamie or Gordon would approve. My idols. I've always enjoyed cooking and cooking shows but never took it seriously. It always felt weirdly below me. I was destined to Excel, not to wear a dirty chef's jacket and sweat over a hot pan, despite it probably bringing me more joy and happiness than a formula or a pivot table. I put on some Cardi B as the eggs are poaching to remind me of simpler times, all those three days ago.

Through some weird turn of events, Alexa started making noise this morning saying she cannot connect to the Wi-Fi when the electricity suddenly came back, which means anarchy by lack of tea is avoidable and people are working hard at restoring some sense of normalcy. I felt relieved. I was never ready to live in a world, or whatever is left of it, without power.

It did make me wonder whether it was the government working hard to get things going again. Sure, they might be fascists, but they still need people to produce, reproduce, and consume. They will get to us, I'm sure. Maybe soon enough there will be some communications or they will try to check for survivors. I'm pretty sure they will start in Mayfair first, and work their way around postcodes, from rich to poor. At around one postcode checked per day, I reckon another three days before they reach Hounslow.

It's fine. I'm fine. Mango is fine. We have resources and for once, in three years of living in London, I have had a conversation with my neighbour. I only know his name because a letter arrived here despite having the correct number, so I did the right thing, walked over one late night and posted the letter through his letterbox just quickly enough to avoid detection and an awkward conversation. How I yearn for those awkward conversations now.

Mango is becoming restless, so I decide to get the *drugs* out. Upon hearing the shake of the catnip bag, he sprints towards my legs and rubs himself onto me. In a weird moment of solidarity, or plain boredom, or madness, I bring up a cigarette paper and roll myself some catnip. I lay on the ground next to him, he's huffing, I'm puffing, and our bond is getting stronger. Just two dudes, a little scared, getting high on catnip trying to survive whatever this is.

"Bitch. Food."

He says, staring me down with his paws on my chest.

"Yeah? You hungry?" I respond nonchalantly, completely ignoring the fact I'm seemingly having a conversation with him. Could be the catnip but I couldn't give a flying one, I'm so lonely and bored that I would entertain a conversation with just about anything.

"Dude, food so good. Me love pouch."

"Why do you never eat anything else, dude? I cook good stuff and you never eat it?"

"No pouch no good."

"But pouch is a product of consumerism, Mango. Pouch no food. Pouch just jelly."

"Jelly good, dude."

He proceeds to clean his groin, spitting occasional hairballs.

"Why do you always do that dude, you're neutered and you barely piss. Surely it can't be that dirty?"

"Good lick, clean dick. Never too sure."

I realise at this point that Mango, or my impression of him, will never use fully nuanced sentences to describe his thoughts. Not sure how much he even rationalises at this point. How conscious he is. It's like having a conversation with a toddler who's high on catnip and self-grooming, bound to not be podcast material.

So, I let him be and go back to the window. Gerrard's cat is staring me down. I point the laser at the window and move it across. He desperately tries to catch it with his paws. "Cats be dumb," I think to myself as I blow catnip smoke.

Yasmin loved Mango. And he loved her back. He would occasionally curl up to her and feel protected and calm. At times I was jealous, as it was ultimately me that saved him from that rescue centre, but I also enjoyed seeing him feel content with what was a stranger, to begin with. She would groom him extensively and play with him and I think he misses her too. He did call me a Bitch one too many times, so I wonder if there's any resentment there.

It's an interesting thing about human connection. The rise and fall of relationships, the vulnerabilities we share with others, the images we try to portray at times, and when all is gone, you are stuck with the same self you tried to adapt through the years. Constantly shifting from one shape to another, trying to adapt to new situations or people based on your purpose or what you are trying to show. I can't remember the last time I was naturally me. No special effects, no carefully curated image, or language.

It was probably with her and it felt good. Until the same things that made me feel accepted ended up pushing her away. You get too comfortable being accepted for who you are; you forget to also change and evolve, thinking that love remains constant and what made her fall in love with you is what's going to keep her around.

That's life, I guess, a cycle of comfort and discomfort, love and hate, peace and war. Opposite forces dancing with each other trying to maintain that equilibrium that allows us to carry on with our day and find our solace and escapism in drugs, alcohol, sex, or gambling.

A laser pointer is going through my front room. It's Gerrard.

Do you have a radio? Tune in on 89.6AM.

I remember having a tiny old radio in one of the drawers in the kitchen. I pick it up, and tune in as Gerrard instructed:

"Hello, mate! What about this apocalypse thing then?"

I could not believe I was hearing a human voice again.

"Yeah mate, pretty grim. You alright?"

That sense of hope was building up. The end of the world is one thing, but isolation in the face of it makes it tenfold more unbearable. A stranger could be my companion through these dark times, and I cannot complain. For once, I cannot find reasons to be unhappy.

"I'm Gerrard, by the way."

"Dom. Dominic. Pleasure to meet, despite the circumstances."

He nods. And with the pleasantries out of the way, we inevitably reach the hard-pressing topics.

"Dropping chemical bombs before *The Traitors* finale, am I right?"

"The cheek! I hope Claudia is fine!"

"Ah, Claudia is the establishment mate. Bet you she's bunkered up somewhere still doing shampoo commercials!" says Gerrard, with a hint of seriousness which I decide to brush off.

"Are you okay with supplies, Gerrard?"

"Ah, yeah, mate! I'm always ready. I felt this day would come. Ever since Bartholomew got into power, I knew a day like this would come. He warned us."

He did warn us indeed. Bartholomew was the Prime Minister, elected by a silent majority following years of economic decline post-Brexit. He was the leader of the Make Britain Great Again party, a party that rose in popularity during the authoritarian regime of Donald Trump in America, "elected" for a 5th term now. The 92-year-old yielded so much influence that nationalists across the world made their own Make (insert name of declining economic power) Great Again spinoff.

The funny thing about nationalism is that it spreads globally. You could see Mr Moss every day on TV warning of a new enemy coming for us to justify any authoritative measure he wanted to take. I used to keep a Bingo card of the world's nations he mentioned as potential enemies of the state. Never the US though, our big brother. Before the end of days, I had two full lines.

"Listen, Dom, I need to feed my cat now. We need to maintain a line of sight for all this to work. Meet me back at 4 PM. I do want to pick your brain more."

"Sure thing, see you in a bit. Hey – nice to hear you, Gerrard."

"You too, mate. No worries, we'll figure this out."

Ah, the male confidence. How I've missed that. Something about us lads having this unwavering level of confidence despite the facts. Think I read some fun surveys saying that most men believe they could land a commercial plane with no training, should the pilot be unconscious. I mean, I know I can… but most of my counterparts, I'm not so sure.

Gerrard could land a plane too, I feel. He has some sort of aura about him, being in control and prepared. I mean, he was prepared for this, and I wasn't. I just went about my weekly shopping at Tesco getting those membership points, thinking this week I'll finally speak to that barista who seems interested in a career in finance.

I head off to the kitchen and decide to make a soup. I have some chicken legs and on the mantra of not wasting perishable goods, it's probably best to make this now. Not to mention the ultimate comfort of sipping a hot soup on a day like this. Nostalgic and reassuring. There's nothing a soup can't ultimately fix.

Some parsnip, carrots and onion go in a hot saucepan, add the chicken leg in to burn on the skin a bit and top it up with stock. Let them all sit there for a while, making friends and throw a few spices to your liking to add flavour. This was my mother's recipe for your cold, headache, fever, arthritis, depression, and a few others.

I feed Mango another pouch and proceed to serve my soup. The recipe is saved for another generation. Who knows, maybe mum was right, and it will help heal biological warfare wounds too, assuming we could still farm chicken. Or the very least, 3D-print them.

....

I decide to play with the radio in the hope of hearing from more survivors. I could hear faint noises but could not establish a connection.

If anyone in Richmond hears this, do you know if Kail, the bakers are still okay, can they deliver Avocado Toast?

This is Krishna. From Southall. Is anyone out there?

Is anyone going to pick the bins anymore? I'm not paying Council Tax this month.

Brentford what'sup! How we' feeling about the apocalypse today, eh? This is DJ Nuke bringing you the best bangers to mash your head to, up next Burna Boy…

To hear that many voices again felt reassuring. How many of us are out there, I wonder? Or more importantly, how many have perished? And how the hell do pirate radio DJs resurface so quickly? In all fairness, DJ Nuke is probably the hero we all need right now. I decide to hold his frequency and listen to some rather unclear, yet consistent, hip-hop music. For a second only, you could close your eyes and feel as though life hasn't changed.

……..

It's half past three and I decided to shower and freshen up. Who knows how much water my boiler tank holds and if the water is still running? The service was abysmal even in the good days. I decided early on to ration the water too, just in case, resorting to a shower every two days or longer if needed. I keep the water on low pressure, short intervals. After all this is the same water I boil for my tea and we've already established how losing that would have catastrophic consequences.

I pick up my *8 in 1, Carbon Energy* shower gel. One of the other wonders of consumerism. I always found it intriguing how they market these products in a gendered way. The feminine shower gel always has notes of the fragrances mentioned – Lavender, Pomegranate or Orange – whilst the male ones always appeal to sensations – Carbon Energy, Aqua Sport, Fresh & Ready.

I guess it leaves space for larger commentary on how most men couldn't care less about specifics and seek the end product. Similar to how they market perfumes. How can one tell what a perfume smells like? One can tell, however, that they would want to be like Johnny Depp or that mysterious successful man that women's noses follow around the room after one spray of whatever they're selling you.

Shit, shower thoughts! Been here for 20 minutes now! Got to dry up and go speak to Gerrard.

"Meow. Bitch. I'm hungry. Meow."

"Not now Mango, just fed you, dude."

I rush down the stairs to my Ouija room and pick up the radio. Gerrard is waiting on the other side, a bit disappointed.

"Apologies, was stuck in traffic." I say, trying to not annoy my first and possibly last friend since this started. He chuckles as to accept my apology.

"I have an idea. I think I might know how to get us moving and out of our houses."

"I'm all ears." I say, not knowing exactly how to feel and whether his plans would yield any success.

The house to the left is burnt down. The house to the right might collectively sacrifice soon, and the house across seems like my only salvation and companionship. At this point, however, it's either believing in that miracle or accepting that I will die listening to DJ Nuke and Mango eating my face to the rhythms of Afrobeats.

LAST YEAR

It's been a year now since she said yes and we're not yet close to actually booking a venue. I always thought that a high-earning job means a fast track to life's moments, since money should technically be available, but you never account for uncertainties. My stepping up on the earnings ladder came with a steep rise in expenses. As if one thing is never enough, always wanting more comfort but never truly being comfortable.

Yasmin decided to stop working as she got hit with depression over the past months. I think all of us have to some degree. House prices are skyrocketing while wages increase too slowly, and the cost of living has bitten into our daily lives. I'm conscious that for most of us, the daily struggle is becoming unbearable and whilst I maintain some sense of sanity, I know very well that Yasmin judges me. She now sees me as upper class, equally guilty of causing the troubles of the world while I justify it by saying that I'm just another cog in the system and if it weren't me, it would've been someone else, so I'd rather it be me so we can afford that daily avocado on toast.

Whilst the money situation is tight, I also have my suspicions that her feelings might've changed too. She's less excited to see me come back from work and every time I bring up our wedding day it seems as if I bring up a chore that I signed her up for.

One night, I got us a bottle of wine that cost me only £50 from Mr Patel's corner shop and decided that maybe it would be good for us to sit down and have a chat. I came home and she was in her bathrobe, lounging on the sofa watching left wing commentators on YouTube asking people to "rise to the power". Yeah, rise and be put down. That's the difference between these anarchists and realists. The anarchists call people to action only to be punched down by the iron fist of authority, whilst we realists understand we have a life, we put up with the shit, try to make the best of it and check out when the time comes.

"Babe, I'm home. Fancy a glass of wine?"

"Why not."

I pour her a glass, take off my coat, and make myself a bit more comfortable on the couch next to her. The video talks about this Bartholomew guy. A bit of a joker with clear fascist tendencies. The newest product of an electorate bored of the same binary choice and heavily influenced by saviour voices. I despise the guy but do not see him as a threat, whereas Yasmin is genuinely doom-mongering about him.

"This piece of shit, Dom. He's rising in the polls and getting more and more attention on all platforms. You literally cannot get through a day without hearing his name."

"Yeah, I heard some guys talk at work as to how he's going to set us on the right track. Scary that."

"Like I am genuinely scared. Have you heard his views on immigration? Benefit claimants? I thought the Tories were the worst we could get but this guy needs to be stopped. Through any means."

I take a sip of wine. I share her beliefs about the guy but don't think he's as popular as she thinks he is.

"I wouldn't worry too much, babe. If anything, we're likely to get stuck with the Tories for another 20 years."

"This is no joke, Dom. My friends are genuinely frightened and want to leave before anything like this comes to reality. They may not be able to at that point. Like, listen to this," she says as she turns up the volume.

The commentator shares a clip of Bartholomew Moss outside a bank's headquarters. It was my bank.

"The poor men and women of this country have been kept poor by the international forces. The same international forces that send their hordes of migrants to our shores as part of their plan to keep us crowded and give us their bottom feeders."

"He's calling people bugs, Dom."

"The bugs of the slums of the world shall not, I repeat shall not, take from the mouths of the hard-working Brits. I know that our industry is ready to respond, reinvesting more capital into our economy, for the betterment of all. A vote for me is a vote for British industry and British people above all."

The commentator then proceeds to liken Bartholomew to Trump and his ascension and, ultimately, establishment as the only unquestionable and unchallengeable leader of the US for the last five terms.

"Is this what we want, Britain? Once guys like these get in power there are only two ways they get out: natural death and death by the people."

Yeah, I don't reckon he'll have a channel for much longer. The Tories already started clamping down on anti-establishment commentators, can't imagine what these bellends would do.

....

A few days have passed and Yasmin has remained in the same anxious and depressed state. She started researching the cost of moving to a different country and kept trying to bring it up with me. I always try to avoid it as I feel like she's ready to uproot our life on a gut feeling and I'm not ready to start again from nothing. We have a future here, one that I've worked very hard for and cannot give up on a whim because some fascist is gaining popularity.

"Babe, how do you feel about Spain? Gorgeous beaches, centrist government, lovely food, they do not see all migrants as bugs, they have Sangria…"

Spain does sound good though. But I do not speak a lick of Spanish. And even then, their banking system is abysmal compared to ours; I would barely be able to make 50 pence to my pound there.

"We can go on holiday in a few months for sure."

"How about a longer holiday though? Come on babe, you surely can't be too content with everything going on. You know what I am, who do you think they will come for first?"

I was not content, but I was not ready to lose everything yet. It makes sense why so many unfortunate people come here to seek betterment despite an already unfriendly climate towards them. When you've got nothing, you've got nothing to lose too.

"Dom, I am serious. Ash just called me from Spain the other day. She arrived safely, started to mingle with the locals and found herself a job in a café. She seems happy, Dom."

Ah, Ash, the doom-monger bestie. *"Everything is bad, everyone's a victim"*, Ash. The purveyor of the finest political commentary that always ends up in revolution or leaving the country.

I nod and suggest I will think about it. I wasn't going to.

....

The day finally came. She packed her bags and was waiting for me in the hallway.

"Last chance, Dom. I don't want to do this, but I have to."

Mango curls around her feet, as if in a last attempt to convince her to stay.

"Yasmin, I can't. All I know and all I have is here."

I wanted to cry, but I couldn't. I had got used to the idea that this may happen. I was mentally ready despite how gut-wrenching it felt at this moment.

"Can we not just wait for the election? You'll see it's not going to happen."

He was polling at 35%. Huge numbers. At this point even I didn't believe myself.

"I must do this. For my sanity and my survival. I will text you when I land and I'm with Ash. We'll talk and take it one day at a time. But trust me, Dom, you'll wish you'd got onto this plane with me."

I bow my head in resignation, she kisses my cheek and leaves, leaving the door wide enough for me to see her get in the taxi and for me to have to close the door on her. A strong metaphorical departure.

She never called back but I saw Ash posting pictures of them going out and enjoying a Sangria by the beach.

She seemed happy for the first time in the last year. That gorgeous smile was back on her face and it reminded me of the woman I fell in love with. I was happy for her and her rebound joy. Like a poor kid window-shopping, I was jealous and wanted that. But I only wanted it when it was too late.

....

It was two weeks before the election and Bartholomew Moss survived an assassination attempt by the far left. Some on the fringe believe it was staged to boost his popularity. Unscathed and with a louder voice than ever, Bartholomew was polling at nearly 40% with both the Tories and labour joining an unseen alliance against the man.

For the first time in 40 years in the UK, net migration was in the negatives. Yasmin and a couple of other million people had decided to depart. Bartholomew was promising the great restart of our economy.

"The fat trimming has begun. A vote for us is a vote for a leaner Britain."

DAY THREE

After Gerrard told me his great plan, I was highly sceptical but also out of choices. He seemed confident that it would work and if it doesn't, we can't blame ourselves for trying. I was supposed to meet him at the window around 2 PM.

The prawn mayo sandwich I made for myself does not satisfy me. It normally does but today I have a knot in my stomach. Did this freak make me believe that we might have some solution? What if I get too excited and then it proves to be nothing, or worse, pointless? Why didn't the government attempt anything yet to reach us, but Gerrard has it all figured out? And why do I trust him?

It's raining outside and the drops have a weird green tinge to them. I keep scrolling through the radio frequencies to hear more voices, reminding me of the community we once had.

Anyone out there? I'm on Cumberland Avenue and have run out of supplies. My grandma is very ill as she left a bathroom window open, and I have no medicines left. Does anyone know what to treat this with?

DJ NUUUUKE here, good morning Mad Max London, here are the tunes to get you and keep you going.

Who do we think it was? The Chinese? The Russians? Iran? Connect to 102.4 and let's discuss.

It feels good to see humanity trying to make sense of everything going on. Nothing promising yet, just speculations and among them I'm sure, *prophets of truth* ready to rally up troops behind their creeds. My book is starting to fill up with recipes and maybe I'll ask Gerrard for some contributions too. This shall be a collective contribution, does he even cook or does he just boil water for his Pot Noodles in between games?

....

A loud, distant siren sounds. Many more follow and all of a sudden, hundreds of planes can be heard. I rush to my loft room to check the skies. The planes seem to be flying in many directions and all of them have banners dragging behind them. I grab my phone and try to zoom in on one of the closest ones.

STAY INSIDE DO NOT RISK YOUR LIFE THE GOVERNMENT WILL REACH YOU

Finally, some news from the government. We still have one, admittedly a rather fascist one. I check across the street and see Gerrard with a face riddled with disbelief. I'm pretty sure he doesn't buy it. He seems the type of guy to question everything even when there are no real questions to ask. I make signs for him to pick up the radio.

"I don't believe this, Dom. How did they get the planes up? What do they know, and we don't?"

"They're the government, mate. They're bound to know more than us. Maybe they got warnings, who knows? MI5 must know something."

"Yeah, listen, it's all bullshit, but let's not focus on that. Are you ready to hear my plan?"

I nod and he disappears for a few minutes. He comes back in a full hazmat suit, holding one smaller one.

"What's the smaller one for mate?"

"The cat! I must try it with him first and then I can try myself."

The lunatic. Ready to sacrifice his cat for scientific

purposes and a chance at salvation. Maybe I'm the mad one for not believing in him. After all, he's looking for real solutions and I'm here writing pasta recipes and trusting the government to save me.

"Okay mate, I'll send Bowie out first. You be on the watch to see how he reacts to it."

I nod and that knot in my gut is now standing in my windpipe. My breath is shallow and my mouth is dry. Bowie looks like that first dog the Russians sent into space. He may become the unsung hero once humanity makes its first steps outside and starts rebuilding society. Mango would never do it. But then I'd never send him to the slaughterhouse like Gerrard would to Bowie.

He opens the front door and throws Bowie out before shutting it. The cat looks uncomfortable in the suit but attempts some steps on the front porch. So far, it seems like the lunatic's idea is working. I'm amazed!

Bowie has been out for two minutes and appears to be fine. He's trying to dig the garden and attempts to arrange his body for a number two. All of a sudden, he starts shaking uncontrollably and acting crazy. Is it the gas or the realisation that he just shat himself in his hazmat suit? Gerrard opens the door and Bowie comes in. He goes back to the window and gives me a thumbs up, proceeding to clean Bowie's backside with wet wipes. Our first experiment was a success. I applaud from the window.

"Alright, Dom. Need to clean Bowie up, but this is promising mate! I'm going to patch up my suit and if all goes well, I'll venture to yours tonight!"

Whilst he's breaking the social norms of inviting himself over, I could not be happier to hear those words.

"I'll pack some supplies and we'll be over around 7 PM."

"Awesome, mate, I'll fix us dinner. Do you have any dietary restrictions?"

"Not at all, mate. See you soon."

That was it. The most normal interaction in the most abnormal of times. My neighbour, whom I haven't spoken to before, in true London fashion, has invited himself over. And I'm excited about it. The prospect of loneliness is so dire that at this point I would do whatever Gerrard wants me to. Do I have a crush on him? Is it the saviour element that makes me blush like a teenager and gets me all giddy about him coming over? Or am I just desperate for any glimmer of hope that makes me confused about the whole situation? Nonetheless, I have dinner to prepare and a companion for the end of the world. Under these circumstances, anything is on the table.

I find a small bottle of red wine in the utility room! I must've bought this when it used to cost £10. The same bottle nowadays, *or three days ago*, costs £30. Just a testament to how bad things have turned out to be.

I decided to make *coq au vin* with the remainder of the chicken that I saved from the soup. I will put this recipe in my book too as I'm not sure if the French have survived and if it's down to a Brit to save their culture, then I shall end the rivalry in the most pacifying way – carrying their recipes through the dawn of a new civilisation. And I don't need any *Merci, beaucoup!* All in the one pot right now, bubbling, and after 45 minutes it's almost done.

Ding-Dong

At least he's got the courtesy of ringing the doorbell. I would've thought, given the urgency of the situation and the fact that there's killing gas out there, he would've gone for a crazy desperate knocking on the door. Even screams or "Hurry up" to add to the intensity of the scene. All the movies I've seen depict door-knocking as a desperate action in these types of situations. But no, Gerrard is chill, casually strolling on my pathway in his makeshift hazmat suit with his buddy in his arms.

"Dom, wear a face mask, open the door quickly and shut it immediately after I come in," he shouts from behind the door.

I conform as if I'm listening to the medical experts providing briefings during Covid. I reach for the doorknob and stop to ponder for a second. Will that not allow enough gas in? Is the gas maybe gone? Do we even need hazmat suits at the moment? I shake out of it. No point risking, so I decided to throw the keys through the post hole.

"Do it yourself mate, I'll keep my distance. Don't want to risk it."

He opens the door, slides acrobatically through the narrowest of gaps and in a flash, closes it behind him. Bowie is in as well, in his shit-stained catmat suit, running up the stairs with Mango chasing him. A large suitcase follows him. He's officially my end of days roomie.

"Long journey?" I ask giddily.

"Bit foggy out there, if I'm honest."

....

I serve the food and we both eat with a sense of accomplishment and tranquillity, as if we've just sorted it all out.

"Delicious stuff, thank you mate."

We "cheers" a beer and get to talking more.

Gerrard is a conventionally unattractive, nerdy looking guy. A 25-ish year-old with frizzy red hair and a chequered shirt, always tucked in. He is an app developer and an avid Dungeons & Dragons...master? Or player? ...Wizard? Couldn't follow.

He has been single for many years as he struggles in social environments and thinks the ladies do not appreciate his nerdy, quirky qualities. Amongst many, many theories, he confirms to me he is one of the bird conspiracists. The Birdhists, as I call them. He believes the government, or some elite international function, use birds to control the population through surveillance.

That surveillance must be a waste. A bunch of pigeon bums and sausage roll crumbs. Who can use that in any shape or form to control the population? He also believes the green sky is chemtrails from the jets flying earlier. I choose not to entertain his theories but listen nonetheless. I have missed the spectrum of human discourse, from casual chat to outlandish theories.

He speaks with ardent conviction and passion as if he's trying to recruit me into his fringe cult. Or like that old friend, trying to reconnect with you only to tie you up in a pyramid scheme. I get the same vibes. That was Gerrard to me right now, the only friend in this world trying to get me to buy into a pyramid scheme, if only he didn't believe pyramids were the works of aliens.

I'm sure my disgust shows by now. My self-perceived moral and intellectual superiority is hard to contain through fake smirks, one-syllable laughs and attempts to shift the conversation. The prick does not shut up, however, and I am drawn into the world of the fringes with a front-row seat to the wildest theories. A sort of Ted Talk run by the most obscure Reddit account. Still, I indulge him since he may be the very reason one of these next few days I will leave the house.

"Do you know what I have here, Dom?" he says, as he waves a USB stick smugly.

"Porn?" Please be porn. One of the greatest American exports there is, to be honest. The only place on earth where at 18 you are old enough to be involved in a filmed gangbang and treated as an object but not old enough to buy yourself a beer after.

"Documentaries. 100+ hours of them. Thought we might put one on before sleep as we have a big day tomorrow."

"Do we now?"

"Yes, mate. I brought over my supplies. It's time to strategise and find the best ways for us to reconnect with others, find out what is happening and with any luck, start building our lives again."

He said that in classical nerd fashion, "strategise". It's all a game to him. I wonder if that's his coping mechanism or his genuine attempts at making sense of all of this. Either way, it might keep us on the path of discovery and, if anything, he does seem a bit more prepared than I am. A nerd would be good right now.

They have seen movies, played games, and probably read a lot of fiction, which could help us navigate the scenarios we are likely to encounter.

In silence, we proceed to watch one of the documentaries.

It is about the Illuminati and world domination. Gerrard's grinning all the way through and occasionally checks on me, to make sure I follow. I try awkwardly to appear interested and support his weird fascination with the world of darkness and mystique. His keen observations irk me, but in the absence of scrolling my phone or distracting myself, I resort to paying attention.

Some things do make sense, I guess. Or is that what **they** want you to believe?

Could it, after all, be the **Illuminati**?

DAY FOUR

A loud sound of metal wakes me up violently and no, this is not Iron Maiden or Rammstein. I get up from the couch and realise Gerrard is sleeping soundly at the other end with Bowie lying on his belly. Mango is hiding in one of the drawers, scared. I raise the window covers to see a tank rolling by on my residential street. At this point, I do not know if it's a dream, but seeing a tank is not far-fetched in the current scenario. Could it be the government? I start banging the window:

"WE ARE HERE!! HELP!"

Gerrard gets up in a flash, rushes and tackles me like a rugby player on the ground. His face looks baffled and his eyes are fixating on me with large pupils, as if he just snorted a line of coke and is about to share an epiphany.

He puts his hand over my mouth and listens carefully as the sounds fade away. He relaxes his grip.

"Don't be an idiot. You don't know who they are."

The tank stops. We both raise our heads ever so slightly, to look through the window. The cultish neighbours start singing songs of praise and hallelujahs. There's a rustling noise for about three seconds and an artillery sound follows.

"Oh my fucking god, was that what I think it was?" says Gerrard, at which I cannot help myself but release a very British "Blimey".

"They shot the freaks – that is murder."

The tank then proceeds slowly, keeping in line with the new 10 miles per hour residential speed limitations introduced by the council in a bid to save lives from speeding. We get up, confused, unsure what to think of what we had just heard and seen. Sure, we didn't like those neighbours, but did the government just shoot its people? What if this is the enemy, and a full-scale invasion is taking place? I look at Gerrard and for once, he does not have a theory.

"If anything, this shows you can't trust anyone. Come on, let's go to the drawing board."

He says that as he pulls up an A3 map of our borough that he brought in his bag, as if that's something that people just happen to have in their house at random. He gets out three miniature ships, presumably from the game Battleships, that he starts to place strategically around the map. I feel like Hitler with his generals in the last days of the Reich with the enemies at the gates, conferring the plan of action, with Gerrard being my Himmler. Or vice versa – I seem to be in the following rank here. Hounslow is our Berlin now.

"Tomorrow, we've got to head out. We can't just wait to be seen by these tanks, whoever they may belong to. We got to go underground. Whatever gas this was, gas goes up – which makes me think the underground should be safe by now."

This all sounds sane and makes sense scientifically, but what makes me doubt it a bit is that its coming from the one who believes birds have cameras attached to their chests like police body cams.

"But I don't have a hazmat suit, and neither does Mango and I'm not leaving him behind."

"Meow Meow. Bitch." – he responds in agreement.

By now, I know that the "Bitch" implies dissatisfaction with one's hunger, so I proceed to grab one of the few remaining pouches of meat mish-mash to serve, whilst Gerrard is drawing paths on the map.

"Listen, Dom. I will sort you one out. I got some material at home. Now, do you have any experience in hand-to-hand combat?"

I thought hard about this. Most of my battles were in boardrooms and occasionally in Facebook comment sections. I loved sharing my opinions and defending them. I was in a couple of fights as a teenager, but most of the time at the receiving end. However, I did take note of the successful strategies of my winning enemies. Beat me once, shame on you. Beat me twice, shame on me. By the third time, I know your moves.

"I have dabbled a bit in the art of fist fighting, yes."

"Ok, I'm an orange belt in Karate. I can teach you a few techniques this afternoon. We need to be prepared for any situation, whether it's militias, aliens or the sorts."

The sorts is what scared me.

"Sounds like a plan, mate. Ok, meet me back here when ready. You have the keys."

He shakes his head approvingly and gets in the hazmat suit. He leaves Bowie under my supervision and proceeds across the street. Both Bowie and Mango now stare at me as the sole provider. I open the fridge and chuck Bowie a bit of salami. With some leftover mash, I decided to fix myself a quick lunch of IKEA-style meatballs.

I wonder what the post-apocalyptic IKEA would look like. What would the furniture of the *Commune* be? Would we make our own? Would we even need such luxuries or would the floor serve as chair and the bench as bed, and is that everything that man will need to see the day through? No more weird *gadgety* furniture for 11 levels of spices, ottomans or foldable chairs. Nothing folds in the *Commune*; comfort is a capitalistic illusion to engage society in a relentless pursuit of better and an endless spend, only to end unsatisfied. Our new purpose will be to survive and be useful in alleviating each other's struggles. Doesn't sound like a very comforting dream, but it does make sense.

I eat quickly and jot down the recipe in my book – thank you Swedes. I chug down a large glass of water and release a satisfying "ah" to confirm the quench of thirst. It's been a few hours and Gerrard hasn't come back yet. Another tank drives by, surveying the area. I left a few blinds open to not be inconspicuous. The tank fires two more rounds at a couple more houses down the street. It all seems random and I can't help but wonder if they're actually just flattening the neighbourhood. And if so, for what purpose?

I'm starting to get worried as I don't know if I'm next, or when will I be. A couple of jets fly by at the same time. The UK has made so many enemies recently with our PM's comments that at this point I've lost all hope in trying to figure out who might've decided to retaliate. I can't even tell if the jets are ours. The planes flying telling us to stay inside were surely ours. Or were they? You can never know. It was such a simple sentence, it could've just been the enemy trying to keep us under control and unassuming.

The wrangling of keys in the door disrupts my thought process. Gerrard is genuinely distressed this time and rushes into the house. He takes off his hazmat suit and comes into the kitchen, pacing himself in an attempt to calm his thoughts, I would think.

"You okay, mate? Have you seen that tank?"

He walks around chaotically now.

"What if…hear me out… this is civil war?"

"What do you mean, mate?"

"Like… what if… the army has decided to support the government and install a military dictatorship? You saw those new generals. Same as the MBGAs! All about power and supremacy! You know how they made those not loyal to them dead meat!"

"I follow you mate, but wouldn't you think they'd be on the people's side, maybe? It's their oath and despite their loyalty to the PM, they are loyal to the people first. I don't believe they could come against us." Although, I was starting to think that they might.

"I don't know man, I don't know. I don't know, I don't know, I don't know…" he keeps repeating that whilst sat down, swinging back and forth like a paranoid pendulum. I put my hand on his shoulder in an attempt to hold him and bring back some sense of clarity.

"Listen, whatever it is – we move tonight. Whoever they are, it looks as if they attack houses where they see movement. For now, this house appears empty."

"Mate, that could've been my house. With me in it!"

"I know. But no time for that now. Let's plan our route, exercise some karate kicks and get suited up after midnight."

In a bizarre twist of events, I have become the rational one. I always manage to find the power of resilience when I see others crumbling around me. I might be the most anxious man in the room, but if another is looking a level higher than me, I shall do my best to console them and in turn, console myself too.

I bring in an old mannequin from the dressing room. Another one of Yasmin's prized possessions has somehow transferred ownership to me despite my multiple requests not to have them in the house. She had a moment when she was into fashion and bought a lifeless mannequin that many times over gave me the fright of my life as she would strategically place it where I'd least expect it. She was fun like that before the depression hit. A prankster and a charmer.

"Here we are, mate. Show me those chops and kicks."

The sight of the mannequin and the request to teach me prove the boost that Gerrard needed at that point to detach from the unexplainable and focus on the apprentice in front of him. With a respectful karate salute towards the mannequin, which I found odd, he proceeds:

"There's a few points you want to hit hard to immobilise the opposition. Here, here and here." He points, going, in order, from the head to the chest and ultimately the groin.

"Got it."

And I start hitting the lifeless body form in a rather unimpressive manner.

"No, no, you need more fire in you. These will be life or death situations, I need you to channel all the anger and resentment you can. Think of someone you hate and let them have it!"

And that's all it took for me to grapple with my anger and unresolved violent thoughts. I kept thinking of this boss I had once. He would constantly blag on about culture, and how we are a family – one that he controlled at every step like a micromanaging paternal figure.

Once, I took a bit too long being ill, and he decided to terminate my contract. So much for the family. Many times, I had dreams of striking him with a karate chop. One of those Napoleonic complex creatures thinking highly of themselves due to a title on the door.

Strike after strike, I hit with precision. My fury knows no bounds. My hands are unforgiving, and my kicks make my enemies shake. The force makes the mannequin crack around the cheekbones and Gerrard joins his hands like Mister Miyagi. I am ready. Bring on those tanks.

"Ok, Bruce Lee. Let's sit down and plan our route. I have suits for you and Mango, all four of us should be good. We need to travel light and hope we meet likeminded others. A backpack each, most useful supplies, and forget about packing too many clothes."

"One pair of each, right?"

"Right! We take out on the backroads. We move through the gardens if we have to. If a street is wide enough to have a tank strolling through it, we don't go through it."

"Ok, let's move at 1 AM then. By then, hopefully we can avoid any detection. We should aim for Hounslow West." I move the destroyer to Hounslow West and continue, "It's harder to reach but your map is old, it now has an underground cover, ever since they made that golf course."

"Smart. Okay, that's clear. Should we try shut-eye for a bit? It's almost nine."

I agree and we move to our separate rooms. I stack some tins and some cereal bars. If it all goes wrong, we can always come back.

Hounslow had become unrecognisable over the last year. Many houses were razed, and infrastructure moved across to make room for golf courses and resorts. For some reason, the MBGA arseholes loved the west of London and saw it as a large green resort for their cronies to relax. Several tube stations have been dug deeper underground to allow the golf courses to be developed.

Hounslow West was one of those places, a whole community shifted around. Deep under, this could be our salvation or damnation, it was too early to tell. We just need to see with our own eyes what is down there and if anyone else also thought to seek refuge underground. They did it in the 1940s, so hopefully that collective memory resonates. It may be a small hope, but the tanks going around the streets surely do not make us feel safe above ground.

. . . .

The water in the cave is really up to our necks now. The candle jars are floating around us, hitting me occasionally in the back of my head. I know how to swim but my hands don't move. All of a sudden, the water starts to drain in a sinkhole effect. As we are spinning, I try to reach Yasmin's hand. She goes down with twice the speed and I follow.

Through tubular twists and turns, it feels as if we are on a water ride at a theme park. The hole with the light is in sight and I get excited.

I pass through it and I'm in a lit tunnel; I keep moving through it.

"Dom, Dom!"

I hear from down below. I keep going but there's no end in sight. The water flow seems to go against me now and I seem to go back to where I come from. I see the dark of the toboggan behind me.

"Dom, Dom!"

I can hear her fading in the distance. A big wave of water brings me and a couple of candle jars back out in the cave. It's all dry and I choke whilst trying to get up on my feet. The cave overlooks a clear, for once not green, but blue sky. Where is Yasmin?

. . . .

I feel two hands on me and an unrequested gaze above. It's Gerrard.

"Get up, it's 1 AM. Pack up and get Mango. We need to move."

SOMETIME BETWEEN DAY FOUR AND FIVE

I grab my belongings and the recipe book on the countertop. I suit up Mango and he looks extremely uncomfortable. That round aquarium-like helmet will surely protect him, but he looks like an astronaut – a catstronaut – ready to embark on a perilous mission. Through a makeshift dispenser, we arrange enough doses of catnip to feed into his and Bowie's nose to have them knocked out enough until we reach Hounslow West.

I pick up the suit that Gerard made for me, in bright yellow, and start zipping it up. I've got two holes for my eyes, protected by glass lenses and a hoodie that is extremely pointy. I check the mirror, as every millennial does before leaving the house, and there I am. A banana if it were a member of the KKK. With an extra K for the potassium.

"Gerrard, what the fuck, man?" I react to the shocking sight of the suit.

"That's the only material I had, man."

"I look like a banana supremacist!"

I was angered but I tried to see the bigger picture. If anything, this could be my last chance at finding better refuge before the next tank shell ravishes my living room. He clutches the doorknob, with Bowie in his other hand and a rolling pin tucked under his armpit. I got the short straw, so I only have a cast iron to defend myself. One heavy hit, though, and you'd leave someone's face medium rare.

"Let's go, lad. Time to shine."

The door opens and a bright light blinds us. In my mind, it feels like the gates to heaven. I expect to be welcomed by some saint, telling me to queue up orderly and to receive my judgement.

I'm sceptical about my order in God's good book. I give out occasionally to the homeless but have probably been responsible for many more homeless people through my job. I try to not waste food but I'm still guilty of ordering a takeaway after doing my shopping. And we're still unclear on his stance on homosexuality – I kind of made a lot of gay friends living in London. If the fundamentalists were wrong, maybe this is the golden ticket.

I take my first step out and my legs have turned to jelly. I need to regulate my breathing as I'm hyperventilating.

"Think of a happy place," I say, as I scout my surroundings and the destruction around me. I start thinking of summer before Covid. Life was so simple and full, and we had the best weather. Picnics and barbeques outside, late-night drinks in the garden. Affordable rents.

I slowly follow Gerrard and realise I've been out for one minute and have not passed out. The nerd did it! His suits work. Thank God for nerds and their undying interest in the sciences and science fiction.

"We need to step it up, Dom."

And thus, we did, slowly meandering through the lanes of Hounslow. Just two men and their two drugged-up cats. I bang my feet over an abandoned scooter – "Fuck" – the pain radiates in my shin. These horrible pieces of technology introduced over the auspice of "ridesharing" and climate-friendly initiatives have plagued our city, left on the ground on every street. Remnants of a life before MBGA when we pretended to care about our planet. Unsurprisingly, Bartholomew highlighted this as one of the million things that is wrong with London, and I agreed for once. I just hated the sight of them.

The air feels dense and the atmosphere is eerie. Someone just checked us out from the window and quickly disappeared behind the curtains. In the green dark of the night, I probably stand out like a sore thumb. A shot is heard in the distance and we hurry, crouching behind a wall. Some screams and squeaks are heard further out.

"Are those foxes, mate?"

With one hand I bend my banana tip backwards and raise my eyesight enough to catch a glimpse of what's happening. A gentleman with a nice tweed suit and a rather fashionable gas mask is foxhunting. But how could the foxes survive the gas over the past few days? All Londoners know that they are indestructible creatures, but this beats imagination.

One of the foxes runs, scared, towards us and finds a hole behind Gerrard's side of the wall to curl through. Mango turns towards him and blasts a faded "Meow" before returning to his coma-like state. The fox curls around Gerrard's legs and is shaking scared. In the distance, the hunter grabs one of the dead foxes and heads into the mist of the night. I look at Gerrard in disbelief.

"We need to move, we're probably less than a mile away." He says, unfazed by what he just saw. He is focused.

We start moving and take note of everything around us. Some houses have been shelled down. In others, you can see the psychological effects of this event. Messages written on the windows, white flags or flags supporting various terrorist organisations in case one of them might be behind this. Kudos to them for trying, I guess. One house even has twenty-odd different nation flags plastered on the main windows with the text "Friends of:" above them. Ah, they just added the Turkish flag too. It's like the United Nations of Paranoia, my type of people!

A few squeaks can be heard behind us. I turn. It's the fox; he's been following us.

"Come, Jamie, keep quiet."

This man has named the fox and has domesticated it in the space of half an hour. Who is this Gerrard guy? Seems like a modern-day Dr Doolittle with hints of Indiana Jones if he worked in software development.

"Jamie? You named it already?"

"Yeah, I just saw him scared and offered some catnip. Seems to work."

Jamie Fox. Two men, two cats and Jamie Fox staring the apocalypse head-on.

The corner shop has racist inscriptions written all over it. But that's been there for a while. We should have seen it. All these fascists hiding in anonymity have been revitalised since the election. I guess you never really know your neighbours. I wonder if Gerrard is one:

"Poor Mr Patel – always the biggest smile on. You shopped here, Gerrard?"

"Yeah mate, he always gave me a special on the vapes. Love the guy."

Ok, that's checked, he's not a fascist. I didn't think he was, but worth checking. Just in case we cross the real fascists, and he throws me out to the wolves.

The sign across points to Hounslow West two hundred feet to our left, crossing a little bridge and walking alongside the golf course fencing. Mango is becoming restless, shaking in my arms, and these are the last yards. We spruce up our steps and cross the bridge in true athletic fashion, like fence runners jumping over abandoned scooters and obstacles alike. We can see the glorious red circle sign with the name of the station in front of us.

Another sign greets us at the bottom of the stairs.

MBGA NOT WELCOME

Ok, we're good for that. We are many things, but fascists we are not. We go past the turnstiles and head down the escalators. The fox is following, and the cats are still high. We rush with each step, both excited to see what's down here. There's that feeling of hope tingling down my spine and my legs turn to jelly again. Will there be neighbours? Friends? A community thriving underground?

We turn the corner and two men in balaclavas are waiting for us. With one swing of the bat, I'm sent to dreamland.

My cast iron falls spectacularly, banging with each side in a never-ending dramatic finish. I look towards Gerrard; he looks as if he's dead. My eyes feel heavy. One of the men is checking my pulse as I pass out.

THE MONTHS BEFORE

It was spring, finally. The past few months have been difficult to bear, more than I would've thought. I miss her and know that she is doing much better in Spain. She probably has a new lover and I hope they bring her the comfort that I was not able to. I keep thinking if I could go back in time, would I pack up and leave with her? Hindsight is a wonderful luxury, an unaffordable one.

Things are getting much worse here and I don't see any way out. AI has replaced my job and hundreds of thousands of others. The Church of Scientology rebranded into the Church of AI, venerating algorithms and machine learning. Cryptocurrency has become mainstream, to the point of banks having most of their customer's savings in various coins, due to the depreciation of the pound. I watch my savings go up and down every day.

The election is around the corner and it has become crystal clear that Bartholomew Moss will win. His voice got louder and just yesterday he survived a supposed assassination attempt by the far left. The press have been eating this up, asking the nation to join in prayer for his recovery, and the main Tory candidate resigned from the election, citing unprecedented levels of violence as a reason. In effect, he redirected half of his electorate to an ever-rising Moss.

As a newly unemployed citizen, I started to fear for my prospects under this administration. They made it clear that if they got into power, they would trim the "fat": the lows of society, the poor, the unemployed, the foreign, the disabled. I started doing some crypto-in-blockchain jobs so I could fill out some tax returns and prove my contribution to society. A mere blockchain trail to keep me down the pecking line of deportation or worse.

Many have been made redundant as the new regime deemed very few services useful to this new society. IT workers were crucial to maintaining and developing further servers to host the increase of digital currency and AI automating many aspects of our lives. Mechanics and construction workers were also needed to upkeep infrastructure or support the new builds and vanity projects of the regime. The police, army, and secret services have also received a lot of funding after going through a rigorous project of loyalty assessments, to keep employed only the most dedicated to the cause.

The leaders of the Labour and Conservative parties have slowly disappeared from the scene. After their futile attempt to join forces in the face of extremism, their campaign tours went away silently. A large number of traditional voters left the country at the end of last year as the picture was becoming clearer.

The "British refugee crisis" resounded throughout Europe and given the loss of freedom of movement during Brexit, many countries started shutting their doors to us, making the visa process near impossible. Some folks from Kent even attempted crossing the channel in dinghies and fishing boats, a stark irony to the image that has built up support for MBGA, on the other lane of the channel crossing route. Those that remained braced for the worst. And worst was just around the corner - MBGA emerged victorious with 62% of the votes.

This is a new dawn for Britain. Rule Britannia!

Labour and Tory were crushed at the election by the unkillable Bartholomew Moss.

It's time to write our history and write it proudly.

Just some of the headlines in the few newspapers left. All have been swung towards the MBGA wet dream and all want to be allowed to keep printing. The TV stations showed crowds of hundreds of thousands outside the party's HQ. A chill went through my spine, and I immediately thought of Yasmin. I reckon she's happy for herself but probably crying with one eye, wishing me and others would've listened.

....

In the first three months, Bartholomew made his intentions clear and kept his promises. Migrants started to be checked for documents and proof of income, disabled people had their disabilities reassessed, and poor people who couldn't afford their increasingly expensive rents were given ultimatums to make up rent or be evicted.

Police and army spending tripled, and names of international state enemies were randomly presented every day by the party's communication channel. A sense of panic and imminent danger was installed in the country, with Bartholomew the only strong, paternal figure to hold the fortress. The "unkillable" father.

Phone listening by the secret services became a daily routine. Everyone speaking against the regime, "the disbelievers", were brought under arrest, interrogated, and re-educated in the kinder spirit of nationalism. We had to develop codes to even speak about Bartholomew, and the "Pope" is what most people stuck with. His right-hand man, the "Priest" was Home Secretary Timothy Bertrand. A man equally evil, equally bloodthirsty, and equally fascist. A former MP who swung his party allegiance tactically each time there was a new opportunity.

The national health service was privatised, with a GP appointment costing £300 or two and a half Barthocoins. If any appointment highlighted a long-term disability, the GPs were prescribed, by law, to report them to the Health Ministry for analysis. Analysis of how to get rid of said disabled person or reassign their usefulness.

Landlords were given more powers than ever. Rent was increased arbitrarily, and those who could not afford it were facing homelessness and imminent deportation to the Cayman Islands – the poor, fortified side, unless able-bodied enough to participate in construction sites. There were rumours at some point that some homeless, migrants, and disabled individuals found refuge in the underground lines.

Ethnically owned shops were attacked, sprayed with racist graffiti or worse. The only takeaways that survived, apart from the corporate chains, were kebabs, curry shops, and fish and chips places of course, but they all had to be run by white, English people. You can imagine the blandness of all the food and all the butter chicken a man can think of. Many times I craved a kebab only for it to be spiced with salt and pepper only. The black market for spices was growing and we used to trade behind the big Tesco's in pop-up one-hour markets on a Tuesday.

It was around this point that Scotland motioned an urgent vote for independence that passed with 90% of yes votes. Wales soon followed and both were in the process of breaking apart from the Union. Some English refugees from Newcastle and the northeast fled to Scotland before they shut their borders. Some progressives from Manchester and Bristol flew to Wales. The country was divided, yet the message was clear on TV and in the press – "The rebirth of Britain is underway."

....

I was slowly accepting the reality of the situation. From regular visits from the police to check my house for not harbouring refugees or illegal materials, to stocking up on paracetamol just in case any sign of illness showed. I would walk restlessly through my house like a ghost in purgatory, battling thoughts of depression and paranoia. I felt watched and listened to every moment of the day. At this point, I was sure that Alexa was working for the government, but somehow, I still found ways to reassure myself that it wasn't that bad.

I was still alive, safe and could get by on life's necessities. The same contentment that had me in this position to begin with, when I could've been in Spain, making love to Yasmin and drinking Sangria.

Nobody spoke to each other anymore, which wasn't that new to any Londoner, but the world felt even more untrustworthy. We would avoid eye contact, physical contact, and even dating apps were dry. I'd been trying for a long time to replace Yasmin's memory with some rebound action, only to find a once diverse dating scene replaced with the monochrome that was now proudly spewing racist views. The dating apps also became increasingly wealth-driven, with joining prices rising each month. I couldn't keep up.

The great dating app exodus made me feel even more lonely; some of my friends from other countries were giving me pity and no one wanted to visit. Britain was slowly becoming a rich-only ethnostate and even those that supported it found it hard to afford living here anymore. Relationships had turned cold and people were just waiting to see the brighter side of things, hoping all the government had done so far had been with some sort of purpose, as if the light was at the end of the tunnel and after all the horrible, nasty things we have accepted as a society, the land of prosperity was awaiting us.

The only thing that kept us together somehow was the entertainment industry, the only one we felt comfortable discussing or even engaging, in the little small talk we did. The greatest show that was running on TV was *The Traitors*, a murder mystery show where traitors are infiltrated in a group of people who try to win a large crypto prize through various challenges as a team. In the end, if there are any traitors left, they will betray the group and take all the money.

But, of course, the party decided to infiltrate some propaganda here too, making the "faithful" believers in the MBGA cause and the "traitors" enemies. The game script was flipped on its head with politically infused paranoia and social commentary proscribed by the party among the lines of "*the traitors cannot destabilise our society*", "*we are stronger when we believe in the cause*", and "*if the traitors win it will be the end of us all*". It still made for good entertainment in bleak times.

....

Last week, I celebrated my 31st birthday with a handful of people, having brunch and overpriced prosecco. The marking of the event has been so insignificant that at this point I'm happy to let time pass by and just guess what my age is. Life has started to move in a monotone rhythm and everything around me is devoid of happiness.

The last months have made London an even more joyless pit of commuters, all strolling back and forth from jobs they didn't enjoy, to homes they couldn't afford, to eat food they couldn't spice anymore. Even Nando's has become "Pope-d" – a term for the collective changes the new administration has brought on to society – serving only lemon and herb and salt and pepper chicken. The migrant exodus came with a heavy price for us *spicy whites*, who enjoyed the blend of cultures and cuisines.

Another Wednesday was slowly rolling by. I just came back from a meeting with the head of a collections firm. They are looking for a claims manager to process debt repayment plans and instruct terms. Once a spat industry, this was now one of the highest growth services in the country, hiring up and down the land. I think it went well, but I feel disgusted. For the past few months, my understanding of the world has changed drastically, and Yasmin's words seem like a warning that I was stupid to ignore. So much for my intellectual capabilities. I feel shameful, as if I signed up to work for the butcher when all my friends are chickens.

The evening is creeping on me, and I am pouring myself a glass of wine. I'm waiting for my Tesco order to arrive so I can start cooking my meal and watch *The Traitors*. We're into the final three episodes, despite everyone knowing the *faithfuls* will win. They must, the party said so. I realise it's dark outside now and I need to get Mango in before the foxes start roaming the streets.

DAY FIVE

"Wake up, white boy!"

I get greeted rather violently by this lady in her thirties, in an accent that sounded Nigerian. I can't see properly, and one of my eyelids feels swollen, but I make sense that she is surrounded by about seven or so other people. My hands are tied behind my back, understandably in this scenario.

"What you doing here, white boy? What's with the racist banana suit, that's a bit offensive, no? Don't suppose you're with the guys wearing the red hats and lost your way around the ends?"

"No, listen," I mutter in a choked voice, "We just wanted to find others and escape the tanks, we heard there may be people underground."

She pauses for a second as if to analyse me from head to toes.

"Okay, okay now, where do poor people belong, white boy?"

"Uhm, where they want to? In their houses, in peace?" I say, worried and hoping I answer in the tone she was expecting.

"What's the biggest threat to Britain, white boy?"

"Uhm… the Pope, the Priest and their cronies."

She nods and a warm smile now follows one of the scariest interactions of my life so far. One of the guys next to her proceeds to free my hands. I feel my wrists and thank them.

"Mango! My cat!"

"He's fine, don't worry. So is the other cat and the fox."

"And Gerrard? The nerd I came with."

"Hazmat boy is fine too – still knocked out. Now, let me tell you how things run around here if you want to be a part."

"Yes, please."

Her name was Patience and she was the daughter of Nigerian immigrants who moved to the UK a few decades ago. She was made homeless during the recent spate of attacks on people on social security. She's lived in the underground for the past month where she met a few of the others that have arrived since. The tube workers knew of their existence but chose not to alert the authorities with whatever empathy they had left.

When the strikes began, they were all underground and heard about it through word of mouth. The noise was enough to keep them under and a radio left in the supply room by the tube workers kept them informed about what was going on above ground. Informed as much as any of us, to be fair.

One of the supply rooms had a couple of gas masks, so at times they ventured out, going from house to house for supplies until the tanks started rolling in, at which point they decided to stay put. She tells me that around 15 people have arrived since the strikes began, taking the total of the group here to 27. She strongly believes, and I have no reason to doubt, that many other underground stations have groups hiding out.

The space they have created has a few amenities to ensure the group's survival. A small electric grill and hob, a radio, some bean bags, and a stack of clothes that people have brought over with each arrival. It resembled my idea of a commune a bit, had it not been under the auspice of extermination. I offer my tins and cereal bars:

"For everyone, please."

Patience approves of the gesture and offers the bars to a couple of kids hiding in the background and playing with a tennis ball. She has a matriarchal aura about her, and the rest of the group seems to heed her instructions. Gerrard gets brought up by some guys and we nod to each other. He looks a bit bruised up but seems able to walk on his feet.

Mango comes from nowhere and I offer him some pats on the head as he rests by my side. We are now sitting in a circle, having some biscuits and connecting around a small firepit made on the platform. A warm tea is served by Patience and one of the guys, Chris, shares his life story. He was a 55-year-old, former Navy with a passion for Sudoku and vapes. The administration deemed him "the fat" and he was released from his part-time duties of assisting with training cadets with explosives. He served in many tours of this country's proxy wars and when the new regime came in, he became vocal about his worries, which ultimately led to his early retirement.

Everyone here has been marked by the events before the end of the world and it becomes chillingly clear that this apocalypse started for most with the election. There are a few children and most of the group looks like they are outcasted by this new society. Immigrants, disabled, and, by the looks of their clothes, homeless. They seem friendly enough, but they all look terrified and you can tell they have been hounded for some time. I guess they weren't as fortunate as Yasmin, to be able to afford a flight and leave before it all went down. Or maybe, just like me, they never thought it could get this bad.

Gerrard takes a turn in sharing his views with the group and most of it is well received. Patience seems interested in Gerrard's theories about the government and his belief that they are behind this. She listens carefully as he goes over his reasons, one by one.

"Yes, they must be. Look around you. What do you see?" she says, agreeing that this was all a plan to make space for the *desirables*.

In fact, what I did see was a decaying society of the have-nots pushed to have nothing. On the fringes, and expulsed even from the fringes that had been drawn upon them. I feel conned by the dream I had been sold for many years and despite being from a different background, I identify with these people so much more than the ones promising to deliver prosperity for my kind. We have become the poster children for broken Britain. Hiding under the carpet like dust.

Most people here escaped the gas, but they had stories of seeing friends or neighbours caught in it. It seemed as though the gas was highly toxic and would affect the lungs immediately. Those lucky enough to encounter little exposure were left very ill and in need of medical attention that no one can afford or access anyway.

Patience offers to cook an okra soup for all of us. I accept graciously and decide to follow her to the cooking space to tell her about my cookbook and ask if I can capture her recipe in it.

"Cookbook, white boy? Are you mad? Who's going to cook after all this?"

"You and I are. And others like us. It's more about our collective memory you see…"

She laughs and picks a pack of frozen okra from what seems to be a small fridge, likely used by the tube workers.

"Okay then, we start by cleaning the okra…"

I take notes diligently and strike up some banter with Patience. I tell her how I am certain that Nigerian jollof is better than Ghanaian jollof and that wins me some brownie points. Ah, the light-hearted hatred for peculiar things we used to have. That used to bring us together.

I quickly realised that Patience's status in this group is dictated by her love for others and how she strives to make this place as homely as possible. No wonder the men, women, and children respect her highly. She is determined, resilient, and strong whilst providing them all a figure to look up to. And within the space of a few hours, and despite her people battering me with a baseball bat, I do feel the same respect and warmth around her.

The soup is done and I sit around a fire with others in the group. We reminisce about the simple things that we miss such as the Premier League, freshly made sausage rolls or Love Island. Jamie Fox joins us and I offer him a bit of soup in a spare bowl. I look in the back and see Gerrard being his nerdy self around Patience. I think she likes him. She seems to chuckle a lot and encourage him further and Gerrard uses this as fuel. I am happy for him. A train is heard in the distance and people start hiding under covers or clothes.

"White boy – hide!"

So, for once in my miserable life, I heed the warning and lay on the ground covered with a blanket. The fire is put out by Chris as the train approaches. It whizzes by us and Patience tells everyone to stay put still. A few gut-wrenching, agonising minutes pass before she tells us we are good now.

These people have what it takes to survive. I might be lucky to be here. One idea springs to mind, seeing these trains running, but I decide to keep it to myself, for now. I still don't know these people and they may not trust me yet.

The atmosphere relaxes and Chris turns on the radio. It's DJ Nuke and he's playing some old Taylor Swift songs. A few of us get together for a dance and Patience and Gerrard exchange a few sweet looks and flirtatious dancing. The epitome of Live, Laugh, Love, in the underground, whilst killer gas and tanks shelling houses are out there. *"Shake it Off"* has never been more relevant and encouraging.

Chris passes me a vape and we proceed to blow steam. I scan the platform properly for the first time and I see Mr Patel and his wife joined up in a hug on the bench. My heart warms up at the sight of him, and I decide to greet him.

"Bossman! Mr Patel, nice to see you here."

He nods but implies he is not in the mood to chat. It hit me that my experience so far has just been marginal discomfort. I'm used to sitting in the house without much happening to me, whereas Mr Patel has had to deal with some nasty abuse over the past months. For me, this is largely escapism from the events above and a sense of adventure and community; for him, this is a bleak reality of a country that no longer wants him. His whole work and contribution to the community, whether it was vapes, booze, Uncle Ben's rice, or staying open until late, has been under attack by the fascists.

If anyone would ask Mr Patel for his allegiance, he would say that he's a proud British Indian with a deep respect for the Crown. A royal family that has not been seen in months, to the point of people speculating they have left the country to be replaced by holograms for the very few public appearances. Didn't matter for Mr Patel; he was the type of man who would die for this country. But to these animals, he was just a brown man, taking too much space in a society supposedly crowded.

Claustrophobia is what they wanted us to feel. Claustrophobia and paranoia.

"Meow Meow. Bitch."

Mango greets me, rubbing his head on my shin and leading me towards the end of the platform.

"What's up, my dude?" I say, as I start following him. Bowie, Jamie Fox, and a few other cats have found a space there. He turns his head to me.

"Meow. Listen, dude. I love you loads but look there."

I look.

"Meow. They're my people, Bitch. Meow."

"I get it, dude, so what are you saying?"

"Meow. I'm saying that this is probably goodbye for now."

I was hurt, but I understood. After all, both he and I were looking for similar things. Community and survival. Would it not be best to achieve that with each belonging where they should? He found his commune and it is better to love and let go, rather than not love at all.

"Well, dude, it's been a journey. I'll be around here if you ever need a cuddle or a scratch, yeah?"

"Meow. Jamie Fox says that there are others out there. Meow. We'll go and bring them over."

If I were Mango, I'd trust Jamie Fox too. The creature survived a shooting and an apocalypse. And, for some reason, it seems that pets can live well above ground. Since I arrived in Hounslow West, three cats have found their way down here. None of them wearing hazmat suits, which makes Bowie's bowel incident yesterday unnecessary.

"Love you, dude, go be free." I say, as a tear rolls down my eye slowly.

"Meow. Meow. Bitch."

And his furry little bum started shaking, his tail was up, and he was heading into the darkness at the edge of the platform. I was hurt, but I understood. Like Yasmin, he had to be where he felt safe.

I return to the group and the discussion fades in the background as I rest my head against the wall. I'm tired and have no idea or care for what time it is.

. . . .

I step out of the cave and the blue sky is empowering. The sun shines brightly.

Patience and Gerrard are running ahead like a happy, enamoured couple, and they scream at me to follow them. I start running. The grass feels fresh and the feeling of it on my feet is calming. As I walk through it, various blades of grass turn into flowers and bloom as if my touch is giving them life. This is proper hippie, but I'm loving it.

"Dom, Dom!"

I hear Yasmin screaming from what appears to be the cave behind me.

"Dom, I'm right here and the long-moustache man is here too. Come back, please."

I want to, but I feel stuck in the ground. My mind wants to go but my feet don't allow me to. I turn to see Gerrard and Patience getting further away and the grass getting greener in the distance. The cave looks dark and surrounded by clouds.

"I'm sorry, Yas, it's my time to go now," I shout, as I start running towards Gerrard and Patience.

All of a sudden, an escalator rises from the ground – I take it, unquestionably, and I'm gently taken up a level to a platform.

At the top is Antonio Banderas, waiting for me. He's telling me I've finally broken free and that the people need me. Gerrard and Patience are waiting for me in the taxi. I open the door and he starts driving us towards the sun.

. . . .

I wake up feeling inspired; it's almost 8 PM and it's the Patel's turn to feed the people. They have this rule where everyone cooks in turns and provides their services to the group. Mr Patel is working on a chicken biryani and the smell is one to die for. Mrs Patel arranges a blanket on the ground and throws a few pillows on it. Chris is on guard duty before me and Gerrard, patrolling the platform and watching for oncoming trains.

Trains have been self-driving for some time now, as per the government's attempt to cut the "dead unionised jobs" and for some reason, they seem to keep running. They do not stop at Hounslow West, however, and they all look empty inside, from what I gathered.

We eat and share a few jokes before it's time for most of us to rest.

People are sleeping soundly around us whilst me and Gerrard are walking up and down the platform – this being the first time since arriving at Hounslow West we get a chance to catch up.

"So, uhm, Patience, yeah?"

He gets visibly shy at hearing her name and looks to the ground.

"Ah, come on, mate. I'm just teasing. She is lovely, apart from having us beaten up to begin with! I saw how she gave you that extra bit of soup at lunch. Or how she giggles at your stories."

"Yeah, she is something else… Listen, how can I like, forge something with her?"

In normal times, I would tell him to ask her out and find out about her hobbies and passions – mundane things. But now, how can one try romanticizing the direness of the situation?

"Be one of yourself, Gerrard!"

"Do you mean, be yourself?"

"No, my friend. Be one of yourself. Whether that is Karate Gerrard, Conspiracy Gerrard, or just Dungeons & Dragons Gerrard. Be someone that she wants to explore and feels comfortable around."

"She is into Dungeons & Dragons too actually, that's what we were laughing about! I said that if I were a mage right now, I would use a spell and…"

He kept babbling, the fool, whilst I just nodded and listened. His happiness is as infectious as it is sickening. I want to pay attention, but I can't; this language just makes me drift on the thin, icy edges of anger, so I prefer to roam around in my thoughts until his story concludes.

"Well, there you have it, mate. Be your nerdy self and she'll catch on!"

"Catch on what, white boy?"

Patience appears out of nowhere. Also, Gerrard is whiter than me, so I'm not digging this white boy tag, but I feel strongly not to voice my opinion, given I did indeed arrived in a banana suit and hence might have been seen as threading on the edges of offensiveness.

"Uhm, we were just talking about nerdy things." I say, trying to save face.

"Go on then, what things?"

A train is coming again, interrupting our chat. We duck and pull the covers over us. This one is going much slower, and my anxiety is increasing – worried that it might stop here. After what feels like a few minutes, it passes us and we get out.

"Okay nerds, do you want some tea?" asks Patience.

Gerrard and I agree, and we go to a different supply room, one I haven't noticed yet, at the other end of the platform. This one has cameras on the outside of the station entrance. The room was incredibly well stocked, including some things that I did not think were needed like tools and guns. I wonder if these are Chris's, seeing as he is a former soldier. He seems like a nice enough lad, but I wonder what made him retreat here and bring his weapons too. Chris comes in with his reusable cup, fills it up with tea, picks one gun and a vape, and heads to take over patrol from us two. Patience turns the radio on.

"Do you do that often? Trying to reach others?" I ask, watching her set it up.

"That, and information. Occasionally we catch others giving updates from other underground stations.

Before all this, we had messaging on our phones. Now with no signal, we only get the occasional messages on the radio."

She scrolls through various frequencies. Nothing too noteworthy – mostly people asking about significant others or families.

Avoid Knightsbridge underground! Heavy military presence – they shoot on sight.

That was on our underground line, several stops further into Central London. Who were they? And how did these people on the radio get there?

"Hello! Hello! Can you hear us?" goes Patience, attempting to make contact. It didn't work.

It dawned on me that if we were to find out some truth about all of this, staying in Hounslow West may never bring us closer to it. I decided to share the idea I came up with earlier with Patience, Chris, and Gerrard.

"Guys, look. I had this thought earlier and I feel right to share it now. If we stay here, we are only in reaction mode, constantly hiding and watching out for trains or whatever military might be coming over. The only way to survive, the way I see it, is to keep moving and, in doing so, understanding what is happening."

Gerrard laughs, as if I'm the one believing the pyramids have been built by aliens. Patience, however, follows me with intrigue.

"Listen, the trains move, and some are slower than others, like the most recent one. I say, we jump on the last carriage and try to explore what's further up the line."

"What about Knightsbridge?" asks Patience, almost convinced to join me in this.

"I guess we either find out ourselves, or we wait until we become Knightsbridge."

Gerrard seems to slowly buy in too. Patience looks around the platform.

"I say me, you, Gerrard, and Chris go for this tomorrow. We have two guns here and a baseball bat. It's nothing against the government's military, but hopefully enough to protect us if we encounter just a handful of people. Plus, I'm pretty sure there are no tanks underground."

"I think we should take some of the explosive materials too," adds Chris. "You never know what we might come up against and we should bring it with us. Not much use for it here."

"Do we have explosive materials?" I ask, dumbfounded.

"We do," adds Chris, "Just some bits that I can put together and make a little explosive device. Nothing too grand, but could come in handy."

I nod and feel energised and relieved I came across these people – they seem like the A-team. Where is my anxiety? Where is my acceptance and contentment? I feel safe here and choose to throw myself into the unknown.

But maybe my safety here is temporary too, therefore moving seems like the best option. Either way, something about Antonio Banderas telling me I've broken free has sent chills all over my body. I feel alive, determined and ready to put up a fight.

DAY SIX

Gerrard taps me on the shoulder and asks me if I want breakfast. I get up sluggishly to join the group and hear Patience explaining our plan to everyone. I unwrap a cereal bar and watch as Mango is chasing Jamie Fox on the platform across.

"Dom!" shouts Patience, waking me up from my trance.

"Yes?"

"Next train, as discussed we jump at the back."

"This is madness," Mr Patel interjects, "you're setting yourselves up for failure. It's a suicide mission."

"Mr Patel, suicide there or homicide here are the same thing. The only difference is our level of control over the situation. I would rather know who is killing us, than not." I reply.

"Well, I know," says Gerrard, "it's the fascists."

"No! The Crown would not allow that," says Mr Patel defensively.

Sometimes, I wish I had Mr Patel's loyalty and Gerrard's imagination. Unfortunately, the last few days have shown me that loyalty is ignorance and imagination serves its purpose in these crazy scenarios, either as medication or coping mechanism.

A flock of pigeons flies through inside the station, and the cats start chasing them. Gerrard screams, lunges to pick up a pistol and starts shooting at the pigeons.

"It's the fucking birds!!!" he shouts as he shoots unforgivably.

"Calm down mate, you're acting insane," I say, as Chris helps me restrain him. "We need the bullets."

"You're the ones that are insane," he says, as he runs towards his victims. He managed to shoot two.

Jamie Fox picks up one with his mouth and takes it into the animals' dungeon. Gerrard comes back with one of them and a rather terrifying smile on his face.

"AHA! See!"

The fucker was right. One of the head-blown pigeons had a GoPro attached to its chest. It's an upside-down world; the conspiracists are right and the sane have gone mad. I take a minute to understand it all.

Gerrard is running around with the dead pigeon shouting "I told you so" and laughing maniacally. I check the camera and look at its footage. It seems like it captured various military actions across Hounslow and Brentford. They look like our tanks, and they are shooting indiscriminately. Could this, after all, be an inside job?

A train slowly approaches and there's no more time for shock or disbelief. This could be the slow train we've been waiting for. Today, we might find out more, or find our end. Either way, we are making a move out of Hounslow West.

We assume positions at the end of the platform. Gerrard cannot contain his smile yet, but he seems focused. Mr Patel sits further down behind a blanket, looking shocked. The racists didn't convince him, but the pigeons did. Funny how we process evidence presented to us. It's all about timing, emotions, and, to some extent, the far-fetched nature of it all.

With each carriage rolling by, the tension builds up. Chris says a Hail Mary and jumps first, Patience follows, then me, and lastly Gerrard. Mr Patel and the rest of the group wave at us encouragingly. *The people need me.* This is the moment.

We are holding onto the edge of the last carriage. The train rolls slowly through the Piccadilly line and each stop has remnants of life all over. We can see the blankets, the put-out fires, the eyes around the corners. We get off one stop before Knightsbridge and decide to carry on the rest of the journey by foot. Noise can be heard in the distance, and we are moving slowly and as inconspicuously as possible.

I'm sweating all over and so is everyone else; the tunnels feel insufferably hot and the equipment we carry – supplies, gas masks, blankets – weigh incredibly heavy. The train has stopped at the platform, and some soldiers step into it to unload some boxes. We hide behind a wall cover and notice large crates being shifted onto the platform. There must've been about twenty-odd of them. A soldier goes on the radio, loud enough for us to hear from where we were.

"Train's departing Knightsbridge, Green Park you're next."

Once the train departs, the same soldier remains patrolling the platform. Gerrard's smartwatch starts beeping, and as he scrambles to stop it, he drops his gas mask and attracts the attention in our direction. The soldier starts marching towards us, using a flashlight to search. Chris makes us a sign to leave it to him and assumes a crouch position behind a panel as if he's ready to pounce, like a lion stalking a gazelle. He was ex-military, a veteran thrown by the system on the streets, he had the know-how.

We retreat deeper in the cover and Chris remains within arm's reach of the track. Once the soldier is close enough, he throws a decoy against the wall to distract him and grabs him in a chokehold. The soldier fights it for a bit, but Chris has that old soldier type of grip. Decades of power in those arms put the soldier to sleep.

"Coast is clear," he whispers.

We join Chris, and I start checking to make sure the soldier is still alive. On close inspection, he appears to be a private militia, with no military insignia or British army imprints. We secure the soldier's rifle and pistol and Patience has him tied up next to the wall. Chris is already within feet of the platform.

"Let's go, follow me."

We move slowly and notice the platform is deserted, yet pristine. No sign of life on the Knightsbridge tube. There is literally nothing and no one to see here.

We go up the stairs, trying to see if it would take us where those crates were taken. We move slowly to not be noticed. As we reach the top of the stairs, I notice two guards watching the main entrance. I make a sign to the group to retreat. Through fortune, we spot a masked square panel.

"It might take us to street level, looks like a vent," says Gerrard.

I agree and offer to go first to check. Chris takes the panel off as I put my mask on, nod at the group and start to make my way up. My anxiety is through the roof at this point. With each crawl, I get closer to the light and the noise, which sounds eerily familiar. I crawl a few more steps and there it is, in the bright lights, the unthinkable.

Thousands of people move around freely and shops are open with sales on full display. A few military men are patrolling the street peacefully, but plenty of civilians seem to be going about their daily lives as if whatever we have been experiencing in Hounslow over the past few days was just a hallucination. I cannot believe my eyes. Where is the gas? The tanks? Nobody is wearing masks, everyone is smartly dressed, and people are sitting outside cafes having a drink and a croissant. I can hear children's laughter and the sounds of busy traffic. Large images are being played on some of the skyscrapers, with Bartholomew giving updates on the *operation*:

The operation is continuing successfully in East and West London, with South and North following. Areas are being cleaned and repurposed for a better life. Your MBGA government thanks you for your patience and cooperation.

Seeing his dumb face with a thumbs-up next to the text made me nauseous. What kind of operation? Cleaned of what? I'm shocked to see people casually strolling by and interacting in the open. A civilian walks past the air duct, so I lower my head, just enough to hear him speaking on the phone. He was looking for property in Brentford and speaking to what I assume to be an estate agent. The reality was slowly creeping on me. I head down to the others as I'm trying to catch my breath.

"Uhm, look, it's not good," I say, noticing their concerned looks. "People are okay up there."

"What do you mean they are okay?" asks Patience, angered and confused.

"There's no green gas and life just looks normal."

"How's that not good?" asks Chris, with genuinely good intentions. "What if they managed to clear the area and are on their way to us?"

"Uhm… looks like a lot of these well-off folks are living as if nothing happened. There is a military presence on the streets, but apart from that, everything looks normal. They are talking about an operation in the East and West with the North and South to follow" I add, slowly starting to realise that to some, the apocalypse may have never happened. A second of shared disbelief is interrupted by an increasingly angrier Patience:

"Like – London? Are they only talking about London? What about the rest of the country? Do they even know what is happening?"

"These fuckers, I'm telling you, it was all part of the plan. The operation is about getting rid of the bugs like he said. We are the bugs. Have always been!" says Gerrard, visibly furious as he rushes towards the duct. To him, this would be the grand confirmation of his wealth replacement theory. I look at Patience and she is lost for words. Chris still does not seem to get it, or rather he prefers not to.

Gerrard climbs up to see for himself. I'm trying to calm myself down and put it all together. Were certain areas better prepared? Did they maybe reach them first? Did they want to reach them only? Was it just an inside job, but then, for whose benefit? The well-offs? The disbelief is slowly being replaced by anger. I keep thinking of Yasmin and the others that forewarned us. It doesn't make sense, or rather, I don't want it to. The thought of being an undesirable creeps in, but not as strongly as the overall feeling of rage at what has been happening to all of us. Again, I see with my own eyes that I'm not what I thought of myself all these years ago. I am in fact, just as much of a disposable as someone living life on the streets once I do not benefit the higher-ups. False illusions all the way, they tell you to climb that ladder, promising purpose and fulfilment, until you find yourself so distracted with the steps, you ignore the ones holding it.

I could've taken the steps onto that plane. Follow my love, and never look back at this desolate society running itself into the ground. *We are the bugs. Have always been.*

"They were just walking as if nothing happened?" asks Patience.

I feel shocked and I find it difficult to speak so I just nod. Gerrard joins us back down.

"I knew it. The fascists were behind this all along." He now walks in circles trying to pace himself repeating "All along" in what seems to be a never-ending approval of his worst beliefs. Truly, out of his wildest theories, a government going after its undesirables was not one to entertain, least when he found out to be one of them.

Patience attempts to calm him down, by wrapping her arms around him. I look at Chris, whose facial expression has not moved an inch. He drags from the vape and looks like he's making some impossible calculus in his head trying to make sense of it all.

"You know Dom," he adds inhaling from his vape "when you join the army, you vow to be on the side of the people. I have always felt that duty deeply and not once have I questioned orders."

"Armies fall in the hands of despots all the time, Chris. It's history repeating itself." I add, trying to console his disbelief at a principle he holds dear.

"What's the difference between killing your own and killing others though?"

Skin colour? Religion? Territory? Resources? Peacekeeping? I wanted to say any of them, but felt like there wasn't an answer he was looking for. Just space for self-realisation.

"I tell you what's the same Dom," he takes another drag of the vape "It's that if you're being ordered to do it, you're expected not to question it."

Some noise can be heard from the station entrance, and we realise it's best to start making our way to the tracks. A train is coming towards us, and we jump on it as the doors open, but we get spotted by a guard joining the platform. He radios in whilst firing some warning shots at us, without any effect. We are on our way back to our world.

We keep passing platforms, but the train doesn't stop. We plan to emergency brake the train one stop before Hounslow West and try to force the door open. The journey back is meek, and we feel tired and shocked by the whole ordeal. Patience has lost her smile, Chris is looking disheartened, and only Gerrard seems fired up.

I read various ads on the carriage. It's all pharma and finance, our top-performing industries. Tech didn't need advertisement as it was everywhere, particularly in the *clouds*. A loan company is advertised next to a collections one. Supplements after supplements all remind you of the desired body and level of health the party wants you at. *"If you're fat, you weigh us down"* says QuickSlim, right next to a digital ad with the latest decrees from the Home Secretary. The disabled seats have been removed from the carriage and replaced with treadmills for the gym rats that want to always stay active.

As we are approaching Hounslow, Chris hits the emergency brake and pulls up a crowbar, starting to wiggle the doors. Patience grabs one end and slowly pulls the doors aside. Gerrard jumps first, I follow, and then Patience. Chris uses all his force to hold the door open and squeeze through. We've got a couple of stops before we reach our base and the silence in the underground allows us to reflect on what we've just seen.

"I say we let everyone know. We start at the base and then we start sending messages on the radio."

The group agrees with me and starts building on the plan. We are now acting as a joint team.

"We need to prepare for any possibility. That soldier saw us and it's likely they have some sort of tracking over the trains," adds Gerrard.

"But the train didn't stop, so realistically they wouldn't know where we were, apart from being on the Piccadilly line."

Chris's point made sense, but at the same time, we have seen the type of force we deal with. Who's to say they do not take each station in turn, cleaning out people one by one? There are people everywhere, taking refuge in tube stations. The weight of the situation starts to press hard on our conscience. Could our actions have put them at risk? What if the response is retaliatory?

And then, through sheer military experience and wisdom, Chris comes up with a great plan. He pulls up the explosives from his bag and starts doing some work around the wires. He thought that if we were to send a train back with explosives by setting up a timer, it could explode close to Knightsbridge, therefore creating either a distraction or a good enough blockade to stop them coming after us.

"Gerrard, give me your smartwatch," said Chris imposingly.

"No way, dude. I need to monitor my heart rate, I get really bad palpitations."

Chris rises and he's now staring down Gerrard. His six-foot-two figure towering over Gerrard's five-foot-seven conveys the seriousness of his intentions. In an attempt to defuse the situation, Patience pleads with Gerrard. He caves in and passes his smartwatch.

"Ok, that's done, what stop is ahead of us?"

"Hounslow East," I confirm.

"Ok, that should mean around 20 minutes journey time to Knightsbridge on the tube, right?"

I nod. A train approaches us from Hounslow East and we go on the opposite tracks. Chris sets a timer and, as the train passes us by, he skilfully places his device on the last carriage. I'm in awe. His plan could buy us a lot of time.

"That should hopefully go off at Knightsbridge."

I give him a tap on the shoulder proudly and we all feel hopeful this could work. This could be our first, small win against whoever we are fighting with. Survival against odds is winning; it's not all about depleting the enemy. Persistence is resistance, I like to think.

． ． ． ． ． ． ．

We arrive at Hounslow West exhausted. Some people gather around us, curious as to what we have seen.

"Tomorrow," says Chris, breaking the group, "now we need to eat and rest."

Mrs Patel greets us and tells us there have been a few new people arriving. Since our departure, Mr Patel went on the radio to let people know of the small community down here, following which about a dozen people have shown up. Gerrard comes up with a plan to relay various signals into one in an attempt to reach more people. He goes into the supply room and starts drawing up some schemes, and Patience follows him inside. Me and Chris have some bhajis that Mrs Patel made for the whole group, and we share a small bottle of wine and a vape.

"I don't know if that worked, Dom. I hope I've done the wiring right."

"It's better than anything I could've come up with, mate. Don't beat yourself up."

"To the end of the world." He said, raising his glass.

"To the end of the rulling class and the prosperity of the have-a-lots."

On the way back, we collectively decided to get some rest and share our findings tomorrow. We are all exhausted and it looks like all of us would need a good night's rest. Telling the group now would make everyone anxious and could lead to unintended consequences. We need everyone to be rested as tomorrow might bring a different faith to this group, if our plan didn't succeed, or worse yet, if those cameras from the pigeons were feeding live to our enemy.

As everyone has fallen asleep and one of the new guys is on guard duty, I struggle to contain my thoughts. The chaos of it all made sense now but the extent of it all was unbearable. The government was knowingly doing this, surely. There is no way an enemy of ours attacks selectively across the capital. This seems like a plan cooked by the most vicious minds of the party. Have we allowed the wolves into the sheep den? How have we been so blinded as to not see their intentions all this time? Did the "have-a-lots" know about all this, and if they do know now, do they care?

I guess none of us, myself included, thought they could take it this far. And those that did think so are long gone. I wonder if people in Spain, or Yasmin in particular, know about what's going on here. Maybe they will put together some international military action to fight off Bartholomew's thugs. Or maybe they have just had enough of us as it is and left us to our self-destructing resolution.

I am restless as I know that we need to act. For once, I am one of the few knowing the truth and it is my moral duty to share it with others. But where do we go from there? Do we just accept it, as it is, once again? Patiently waiting for our end at the hands of a militia or worse, as history has shown us time and time again, we go at each other, embroiled in insignificant conflicts internally and missing the bigger picture.

Time will tell, but the time to wait around and find out has passed. Yasmin's fire has finally lit up in me.

DAY SEVEN

A baby's cry wakes me up. One of the ladies who joined our group the other day brought her newborn with her. She tries to pacify her, but her efforts are futile. I get up and catch Chris reading my cookbook.

"So, what do you think of it?"

"It's a bit random if I'm honest, mate, but yeah, some good recipes in there. Tell you what, when this is over I need to take you to my mate in Paddington. He's running, or used to run, this amazing Brazilian barbeque joint. Meat just falls off the bone."

That sounded amazing. The decadence of indulging in platters of smoked meat is something that seems lost in the glory of the olden days.

"You should make a list of things that people can use in situations like these." Chris adds.

"What, you mean like foods that can be found?"

"Not necessarily, like stuff that people can have ready, in case something like this happens," he says as he starts to write in my book. "Tins of tuna, sweetcorn…"

"Beans!" I say as he keeps adding to the list.

Gerrard steps out of the supply room and joins us, Patience following barely inconspicuously.

"Gents, I think I might've cracked it. I think we should be able to reach radio waves on a 5-mile radius."

That was amazing news. For once, we had a direct reach outside and we were sitting on precious information. I stand up and scout the platform:

"Everyone, please gather up." Wandering figures slowly make a circle around us. The new people stand more in the back and the baby is still crying. "What I share with you now is both true and hard to take. So, I will only do it once, but I need more of us to hear it." People look worried around me. I ask Gerrard to activate the transmitter and he confirms the audio is live:

"My friends, I hope you can hear me okay. And if you can, please pass along this message. Life in rich areas like

Knightsbridge seems to have resumed. People are back to enjoying expensive coffees made by bisexuals and buying Egyptian bed sheets at Harrods – whilst most of us are hiding like rats in the sewers.

"If you're tired of golf courses erasing your neighbourhood, the militias shooting at you, and The Traitors always ending the same way, I ask you to seek the fire to fight back. The Pope and Priest fear us when we are united and the only way they win is if we stay hiding.

"London is for us. The non-small-talkers, the takeaway patrons, the tourist haters. We all came from different parts of the world and made this place our home.

"We, at Hounslow West, have seen the truth. The well-off are guarded by militias and they carry on as if our nightmare does not exist. London is now only for the rich, unless we claim our parks, our corner shops, and our tubes back. My name is Dom and I'm with another 37 souls here ready to put an end to this bloody tyranny."

I pass the transmitter to Gerrard and leave the scene to retreat in one of the supply rooms to gather my thoughts and emotions. I can see everyone remaining still where I left them, unmovable while Patience tries to explain things again.

To some, it is the shock factor; to others, just a confirmation of their worst fears. To everyone, however, the choice became clear, and the pieces of the puzzle were coming together. A hashing noise was heard on the radio:

This is Osterley, Hounslow West. 42 souls here. We heard you and we thank you for sharing that.

Acton Town here – 51 people. What's the plan then?

Similar messages came through. One by one, various areas were responding and even more and more individual households were asking to join the underground stations. For once in the past week, we were no longer isolated and perhaps more connected than ever. As messages kept coming in, some others have signalled more guarded tube stations. It became obvious that there were certain areas deemed worthy of perpetuity.

Patience joins me and offers a hug. We both know that the road ahead has just become more complicated. We don't know if the messages have been heard by the government or if they even care, but we were feeling proud of ourselves. Her struggles over the past few months have rendered her feeling powerless and my constant indecision and contentment with whatever happened to me have led us to this moment where we both found the power in us to stand up in the face of adversity.

For the last hour, I have seen people going from disbelief to anger. Previously, I would've thought anger was a negative emotion. And whilst that may be true in many situations, one in which you are erased from society requires anger to fuel up resistance. Succumbing to our fate would mean participating in our systematically planned eradication.

We hear a train coming and we disperse quickly and start hiding. We shut off the radio and cover ourselves in the darker corners of the platform. The train's emergency brakes are applied and there's a lot of noise coming out of it. About thirty people get out, carrying weapons.

"We come in peace," says one of the men.

"We are from the Northolt military base – Royal Air Force vets. We heard the call on the radio!"

Patience looks at me and begs me not to get up, but I decide it's worth the risk. The militias wouldn't come knocking.

"Don't shoot! It's Dom, from the radio earlier, there's people here unarmed."

They lower their weapons and start walking towards me.

"Sergeant Fowler, a pleasure to meet, Dom. This is Corporal Sandhu. We are from a former RAF unit, displaced a few months ago."

I greet them with a cordial nod and the rest of the people hiding start showing and greeting some of the soldiers. Food is being exchanged and people engage in small talk.

They told us how when the government hand-picked the new order of the army, many were made redundant and lost their jobs. When the strikes happened, they maintained comms through radio. Similar to many of us, they believed it was a foreign enemy as they did not recognise the jets or the gas used.

In an act of camaraderie, a group of them decided to storm the former army base to get weapons and stock up on supplies in case they needed to protect themselves. Apparently, the situation was similar with other bases scattered around London.

The dimensions of the story would start to become more nuanced and confirm some of the news we heard. The government reduced army personnel to a strong ideological base and trimmed "the fat" as promised. On top of that, it hired foreign, mostly American, militias to make what is now the official Army of England. A personal guard for Bartholomew Moss, their cronies, and the oligarchs of England.

"When we fought some of the Americans at Northolt," Fowler tells us, "I dropped my mask running away with the supplies. I must've been exposed for about five minutes but have shown no signs of illness since."

Gerrard seemed intrigued and zoned out as if he was performing advanced mathematics in his head.

"That makes sense, though," he interjects. "That would explain why the foxes and cats are fine. Perhaps we are now, as well."

"That would also explain why they sent tanks in," adds Patience. "The gas could've been the first wave."

None of us, however, are brave enough to go up and test our new hypothesis. The images of people coughing their lungs up a week ago are too powerful.

. . . .

Messages keep flowing on the radio: areas of Richmond, Primrose Hill, Mayfair, the City of London, and Westminster are fully guarded and supposedly thriving based on people's testimonies. Fowler pulls up a map of London and we start making note of the messages and signs of underground resistance. Gerrard joins and brings the battleships that he brought in his backpack.

"I thought we only got the necessities mate."

"Can't leave a nerd without his toys. See, they're useful now."

I leave the military planning to the army guys and offer to cook tonight, using Gerrard's help. The soldiers have brought plenty of food supplies so we are set to cook a feast.

Using a wide, circular platform mirror we ripped from the wall, we put that on the electric grill. Being metal itself, it warms up pretty fast. I decided to make a mushroom risotto using the large batches of arborio rice we have and the dried mushrooms from the army supplies. People come for a serving one by one, and we sit together in kind of a theatre arrangement as Corporal Sandhu has offered some entertainment for the evening. She offered to sing for the group and her voice was soothing, singing songs from better days like *Wrecking Ball* by Miley Cyrus.

Tears were running down my cheeks. Mrs Patel kissed her husband's cheek. Chris was playing an air guitar whilst Gerrard was curled up in Patience's arms, all protected.

For a moment, you could close your eyes and Sandhu's voice would take you to that nightclub that you were so keen to leave but now you wish you'd never. That moment when she looked into your eyes and danced silly around you. The hordes of people heading to the kebab shop after for some greasy chips. The crazy, drunk sex once you got home, hitting your shins on the edges of the bed during the moment and the lousy making out.

The song is interrupted by loud bangs outside of the station. Fowler listens closely as the rest of the group looks scared. I stand up and head towards the supply room. The cameras have been cut off and the noise is constant. A barrage of shells can be heard all around us and the roof of the station starts shaking, particles of dust falling over our heads. The newborn starts crying again and the atmosphere quickly flips on its head.

I take the woman with the baby, Mrs Patel, and a few older folks inside the supply room. Patience decides to stay with the group. Fowler and his guys start distributing some weapons and showing the basics of using them. Aim. Press trigger. Shoot. Gas masks are passed from one to another. The sound of shelling stops and it is a bleak silence.

"Go go go," can be heard as several people rush down the stairs. Fowler starts shooting in that direction whilst I go and hide in the stopped tube with Chris by my side. We all assume various positions in the carriage and start shooting back.

New messages keep coming up on the radio:

We are being shot at in Northfields.

Government troops at Ealing Broadway – be careful.

In all the chaos, the radio gets shot and shut down. A few of the government troops have fallen to the ground. Fowler and Sandhu push their soldiers forward; we stand back for now. Patience comes out of the supply room with an automatic rifle, effectively flanking the government troops. Some motorcycles can be heard coming towards us from the tunnels and it feels like we are being attacked from all sides.

I was not ready for this, yet somehow I shoot as my life depends on it. A former account manager, on the cusp of survival, in the city that made me, but now wants to break me.

ONE OF THE MANY DAYS THAT FOLLOWED

A drop of water falls on my face. It's dark, I'm hurt and I'm thirsty. I find the power to push with my legs and drag my back against the floor, enough for the following drops to land in my mouth.

I don't know for how long I've been down and whether Gerrard had a chance to figure out how to stabilise the radio lines. There have been a few days of intense fighting in the underground – for every win we get, they send more soldiers our way. The situation is similar in other places too. We have managed to push back, but only just.

The government has found ways to disrupt our radio signal and filter propaganda by calling the resistance "terrorists" and trying to persuade people that what it did was claiming back control and clearing the gas one neighbourhood at a time. Fortunately for us, they were unsuccessful and even the least of the believers have tipped more towards the cause, taking the fight onto the streets. Bystanders got more involved in the logistics of survival and the ones ready to fight were more ready than ever.

"Hey Dom, where you at, buddy?"

"I'm by the exit sign, mate. I'm almost dead."

Earlier that day, when we had a respite from the fighting, we decided to venture out to a nearby radio tower, with Gerrard confident he could restore the communication. The soldiers we have killed in the fighting had plenty of resources that we made our own, like vests, guns, and protein bars. We used the weapons for recon missions around the tube station, as well as what Chris dubbed "pantry raids", getting food and medicine to bring back underground.

We knew the gas was not there, but tanks were, so our only viable option was to remain below ground and build from there. This radio tower was unfortunately guarded, and I took quite a beating in a fistfight with a guard that no amount of karate chops could have saved me from. Fortunately, Gerrard helped, and whilst I passed out from the injuries, he went up to the main room to figure out the radio.

"It's good to go now," says Gerrard, with a heavy sense of accomplishment. "Think you can get up by yourself or do you enjoy being a bit of a drama queen now?"

I smile and get up. I was being dramatic but I am also exhausted. For once, I enjoyed the prospect of being almost dead, if it meant a break from all of this chaos.

We start walking down the main road and the atmosphere is different from when we first went out. Now, the silence is cut by sounds of gunfire, cheers, and army jets patrolling the sky. Captain Fowler and his team managed to regain control after guerilla fighting at the Northolt base, and now the army is keeping the sky clean whenever they can, whilst we carry on fighting on the ground. We are not killers and do not wish to harm if we can avoid it, so we engage in territorial fights and try to gain ground and convert bystanders.

"Mr Patel's shop!" I shout, as we go by the corner shop that stands out in its bright yellow colours in this grim décor. "Shall we go in? Get some vapes for Chris and see what else?"

"Yes mate, let's go for it."

The bell still rings as I open the door. Of course, it does. The packets and boxes of crips by the entrance look as enticing as ever. We grab some chocolates from the tills for the young ones back down.

"Dom – check this."

I follow him behind the till. He holds a picture of a young Mr and Mrs Patel in front of the shop. It was hidden behind the counter. I almost teared up. This is not the future they would've thought for themselves when they set this up. A shop graffitied by fascist symbols and a country gentrified from within with chemical weapons. We take it with us, alongside the chocolates and vapes, and we head towards the station.

We are now more than one hundred on the platforms of Hounslow West. People have brought on more supplies, but we are conscious this is not a long-term solution, and we need to intensify our fighting and claim back more control. I gather Chris, Gerrard, and Patience in the supply room.

"Guys, we need to push more centrally to put pressure on the government. I say we get in touch with the Ladbroke Grove guys so we can push on Notting Hill. It seems like the type of area that would be protected by the government."

"Are the comms working?" asks Chris. Gerrard scans some frequency and we hear the static and some voices on the other end.

I pick up the transmitter – *"Ladbroke Grove – do you copy? This is Hounslow West,"* – silence.

"Ladbroke Gro…"

"Mr Hero! Nice to hear from you – yes we are here still – about 150 souls."

"Good to hear! Armed and ready for a fight, if needed?"

"No time better than now, Dom – There's heavy military presence on Portobello Road, something tells me some Russian oligarchs have some high-value assets they need protecting."

Another voice intervenes:

"Uhm, Hounslow, Ladbroke, sorry for eavesdropping – Shepherd's Bush here. We don't want to miss any of the action."

And neither did Kilburn. Nor Willesden. The sheep have decided they would rather go inside the slaughterhouse to fight the shepherd. It was inspiring to see so many keen to take on the fight, and if momentum was anything to go by, what a fight this would be.

"Sounds like we're in for a treat! We'll be with you tomorrow, Ladbroke, sleep well tonight." I drop the transmitter and look at my gang. A mix of excitement and fear is clearly what's on their faces now. I sit down, take a long drag out of a vape and exhale.

That night, we played charades and laughed at Gerrard's depiction of Bartholomew. Even Mango and the crew decided to join in the action. It was Chris's turn to make some food and he decided to go with burgers, with the smell irresistible to even the most indifferent of animals. I gave Mango a few pats on the head and passed him a bit of meat that he chose not to eat, of course. But I think he had missed my presence, a bit.

....

The sun is blinding me and I can almost hear the sweat drops touching the sand. I'm smoking cigars with Antonio Banderas and the waves come crashing near us. I'm sunk in the sunbed and I'm sure the gaps in the plastic will leave red marks on my back but this Sangria in my hand is to die for.

"Mr Banderas, is it not hard being a hero to so many?" I ask him in admiration.

"A hero is not born, they are made."

"No, I get that, but I feel that many people look up to me now and I'm not sure if I'm the person they should do that to."

"Heroes are ordinary people who make themselves extraordinary," he says, as he drags some deep cigar smoke.

I ponder what he says and how he's not really answering my questions, but he's Antonio Banderas and I'm Dominic Hargreaves. Who am I to question a genius?

"Are you never afraid, though?"

"FEAR has two meanings. Forget Everything And Run or Face Everything And Rise. Choose yours."

At this point, I'm fed up with his speech bubbles and realise my hero is just a talking cliché. Like a motivational speaker that nobody wants to hear anymore, recycling the same material that makes happy clappers pay money to feel a sense of purpose packaged in cute sound bites when everything they heard was already within them. You don't need a charlatan to tell you things you know but choose not to believe. The hero was already in me, I just needed to seek him. I am Antonio Banderas.

I take another sip of the Sangria and get off the sunbed. My back hurts and I look like a pink zebra.

"Go fuck yourself, Antonio Banderas."

....

Around 30 of us are ready to leave towards Notting Hill. I glance over at Patience and Gerrard engaging in a bit of pre-fight affection. Chris is checking his weapon diligently and seems extremely focused. Mr Patel is approaching me slowly:

"I think I want to join this, Dom," he says, with a shaky voice.

"Mr Patel – there's plenty of us – there is no need. I'm sure the group needs you here."

"Dom – when you brought this back to me," he says, as he shows me the picture of him and Mrs Patel, "it reminded me of how much I care about this country and how much I want to fight to get it back."

I want to insist on him not coming but I can't. Who am I to decide what is worth fighting for, for anyone? I don't blame the bystanders. I don't even blame the militias. We all have something at stake here, and to some, that desire is more powerful than the prospects of death.

I blame the government, for creating this situation, this Armageddon where we are pitted against each other, fighting some poor mercenaries brought over with money to fulfil this deranged utopic experiment for the wealthy. One that we hope to bring closer to an end today.

"Gear up then, bossman," I say, as I see Patience now talking to the group that will stay back and providing them with rations and suggestions for use of resources whilst we are gone. Mrs Patel is to be left in charge, as one of the first settlers in Hounslow West, and she's given a radio transmitter so we can be in touch throughout.

"All right gang, the sun's rising soon, we need to move," says Chris, as we say our goodbyes to those left behind. We head into the dark tunnel. There's an hours-long journey ahead of us.

....

"We are under fire hurry up," we hear on the radio as we approach the steps of Holland Park station. The sound of gunfire is increasingly louder and the air weighs heavy on my chest. Chris, used to decades of vaping, runs

through the thick smoke towards cover like an athlete in his prime. We follow and take refuge behind a double-decker heavily assaulted by machine guns.

"We need to flank from the left," says Patience, in between glances through one of the windows. The constant sound of bullets being fired is deafening.

I decided to make a jump at it and run behind a black cab to the side of the bus, shooting in the direction of the militias who were barricaded inside various large houses outside of the station. The sound of tanks can be heard rolling towards us from the distance. The Shepherd's Bush battalion is trying to draw fire from the right. A couple of their people have been shot and are calling for help, trying to hide from the storm of bullets. This is chaos. Brutal chaos. I miss my old life.

Gerrard comes crouching by me, and as Chris and Patience join us, the double-decker is being blown to pieces by the shell of a tank, now within a hundred feet from us.

We radio in – *"We really need help, we are outside Holland Park station taking fire from all sides."* I see Mr Patel being hidden behind an advertising screen. He seems scared but not willing to leave without a fight. He returns a few bullets towards a balcony and ducks back. One shot, however, finds its way into his leg. He falls, struck, to the ground. I rush to help him when all of a sudden, a dozen planes cross the sky, dropping bombs over the houses. The explosions have us all ducking behind any sort of protection and the whole ordeal lasts around 30 seconds. It feels never-ending.

The dust is starting to settle, the smoke is black and dense, and the silence is only broken by moans of pain and coughs. I move my hand across and feel Gerrard. He tells me he is okay and Patience confirms too. A soldier picks me up and I can see the flag on his uniform; he is army.

"You ok mate?" he asks, but I can't see his face.

"Yeah, thanks. I guess those planes were ours."

"Damn right, the goddamn R-A-F!" he says, as he proceeds to pull Patience up as well. "We heard your radio, we decided to come help you out. There were large numbers of militias there, and a victory for you is a victory for us."

I take a moment to regain my senses and check the area when I see Mr Patel, lying still.

"Dom, can you hear us – we heard explosions are you guys

ok?" can be heard on our radio.

"Stand by Hounslow West – we'll be in touch soon," I reply.

I bend down to check on Mr Patel and he is not breathing. I try some CPR for a few minutes but to no avail. He is gone. I feel proud more than I feel sad, weirdly. I'm concerned about Mrs Patel and breaking the news to her, with her only comfort being that he died doing what he wanted. And what he wanted was to be free again. If there is anything that Mr Patel has shown us here, it's that standing up for your beliefs, even in the face of death, is the ultimate act of freedom. Patience joins me with tears in her eyes and puts her arm around my shoulder.

"I'm so glad I got that Biryani recipe from him," I tell her as she covers him with a jacket.

Chris approaches tearfully and places a vape on his chest.

"Thanks for everything, bossman."

In the silence of the aftermath, we pay our respects for a moment, and then start grabbing whatever supplies and weapons there are left. We don't know what's around the corner, so our time for mourning is, unfortunately, limited.

....

We carry on alongside the soldiers, house by house on the main road, checking for people and militias alike. The night finds us in the vicinity of Hyde Park, where we decide to separate and return to our bases.

Today was a good victory, but at a big cost to all of us. We will bring Mr Patel and others back to Hounslow and then get ready for a possible government retaliation. It always comes when they lose a battle. Everyone can feel it though, that the government is bleeding. They are on their last legs now; it might be just a matter of time and determination, but our numbers are growing each day.

On the journey back, I think of Mr Patel and the others I have met on this journey, and how much our lives have changed. But most importantly how our relationships have changed. We went from being inside our houses, even before the gas, nonchalant to the world outside our walls and too preoccupied with our wealth, health and joy to standing up together, finding community in the darkest of times.

Those constant reinforcements of "others" coming after us, to ruin us, to hurt us, were all a psyop to get us content, disjointed and wary. Spending was the only thing that made us happy, and protecting what we spent was our purpose. Everyone had an outside world they were fearful of, without realising it was in fact a shared world. One that, if we were to step into, we would find others like us.

It took us one apocalypse to find that out, but in the end, we found each other.

DAY TWENTY-EIGHT

At the last count, we were at least one million. The army guys have helped us organise and to get this far without their help would've been impossible. I guess it goes to show that you can't just rely on mercenaries and sometimes the *fat* you just *trimmed* was the glue that kept it all together.

Some of the assaults on the ground have been bloody, and we lost some fights, but with each fight above and underground, our movement gained more and more followers and awareness, and the most unlikely characters were ready to take arms. I say that as I look to my left at Mrs Patel, tightly holding a carabine and ready to push alongside us. Chris is chewing gum loudly in my ear and the intensity of what's next can be felt at the tips of my finger softly touching the gun trigger.

"Ok, let's go," I instruct Chris and Mrs Patel.

We are at Westminster and our goal is to ring the Big Ben tower bell. Parliament is heavily guarded, but artillery secured by the resistance is shelling the area heavily, therefore we can move rather incognito. Two soldiers come towards us and Mrs Patel headshots one whilst I disarm the other. Chris throws the grapples onto the clock and slowly lifts himself upward. I follow, and Mrs Patel keeps watch on the ground. A few weeks of intense battles have turned us into prime SAS troops. And in finding my voice and my principles, I have become one of the leaders of the resistance.

Gerrard and some other nerds have managed to restore the internet signal through whatever nerd magic they got up to. It is, however, very patchy, and we can only activate it for a few minutes. Him and Patience are waiting for my signal to livestream the moment.

The *Commune of Hounslow* has the largest following on TikTok at the moment and hundreds of thousands are waiting for the livestream to come on. This can be our V-Day moment. If only everything goes to plan.

. . . .

The past few weeks have seen us gaining small ground across the Capital. Similar movements have organically brewed in other cities across the country where the government military has taken a presence to isolate communities and stop people finding out about London. The narrative was all about terrorists taking over and the government dealing with it. In the absence of a means of communication initially, the situation has shown us that we don't need some figurehead to tell us when "enough is enough" and sometimes, we can all just feel it and find ways to organise locally and seek one another.

Through the radio comms, we shared our realisation of the gas no longer being present and many fights have been carried on the streets. By sharing the government's plans, we inspired other groups to act locally. The resistance had small, albeit important, strategic wins across the capital and the largest cities. The government couldn't keep up with the number of fights all over.

The Home Secretary's assassination whilst he was doing a PR stunt at Greggs last week was a stroke of genius from Fowler's mates. All sausage rolls that day had been poisoned. He fell sick hours after and died at the hands of private consultants at the Chelsea Hospital.

More and more information went out about the state of London and the government's attempt at redrawing the borders of society. Rich areas had been selectively protected by installing ventilation on the streets to help keep the gas at bay in the early days. Select members of the party and its supporters were given forewarning and gas masks if they were to stay within the undesirable areas. The plan was for London to become like the Cayman Islands, the rich side of Europe's wealthiest, with eradicated neighbourhoods being used as blank canvases for vanity housing. The country was to become an airport terminal with little infrastructure to provide living conditions unless you had a jet or a helicopter, becoming a fuel stop for flights between the US and the rest of Europe and Asia.

The remaining hundreds of thousands of workers were to be kept on minimum wage and allowed to keep their properties to ensure some services functioning for the elite. But the biggest news that struck everyone was the revelation that Bartholomew Moss was just an AI-modelled humanoid, produced by Silicon Valley's brightest minds. It became apparent once the livestreams started pouring in and some resistance workers attempted to injure him by throwing acid on him, only to reveal robotic circuits behind his cheekbones.

Despite all the shocks, our mission was unwavering and our intent to regain our freedom was never stronger. I was flabbergasted by all the twists that had unravelled before me, yet I found the strength to remain an influential figure in this fight.

And get this… Yasmin commented on one of my livestreams with "Viva la revolución" and a heart emoji. Now, I'm not trying to get my hopes up here, and I'm definitely in a better space months after seeing her, but it did act as a necessary boost as I grasped the new realities. I went from leaving the house with a cast iron ready to bash someone's head in, to climbing Big Ben and sounding the start of the attack on Westminster.

On my way to the fight at Chiswick House, I came across a BBC producer who spoiled The Traitors finale for me. Of course, the "faithfuls" won and Claudia was indeed sheltered by the authorities and the shampoo industry.

The last MBGA cronies tried attempts at negotiating with the resistance, offering us Essex in exchange for ending the hostilities.

"Nobody wants Essex," said Ed Downy of the Kingdom of Hackney at the negotiations, slapping the MBGA commissary, and shooting him in his eye socket. That made for a great video.

Four weeks ago today, I just did my final Tesco

shopping and was contemplating the green sky. Ah, you won't guess what that was. Because of our speeding up of climate change and the increased humidity, the gas rose up and created this green-like thin blanket across the atmosphere which – get this – they would use as a green screen to project satellite pictures to the outside world with everything looking fine. Google Maps was in on this too, earning a very nice contract on the back of our suffering.

To the rest of the world, London was fine and carrying on its mundane existence. Once videos on the ground started going online, the world took note and protests were held in every capital. The UN held 20 different general assemblies to stop this genocide, but of course, the US vetoed on each occasion claiming the government had a right to defend itself from terrorism, and no resolution was ratified. We were left alone, but we were not alone as support reached us in many different ways. From weapons to servers to maintain our signals, the world came to our aid and was cheering for us on the socials.

Gerrard and Patience's love through all the fighting has already been picked by Japanese creators as a source of one of the finest British-inspired anime. A guy in

Lithuania loved my cookbook idea and decided to create a website for it where people around the world could cook the meals from my book and we'd receive donations from supporters willing to aid our cause. Gordon Ramsay, now a refugee in Malta, wrote to me and wished me strength and resilience.

. . . .

As I climb towards the clock, I become mesmerised by the blue sky. I push through each difficult climb and reach the top with Chris. The view is breathtaking – you could see very few patches of green sky in the distance and now a shelled-up Westminster bridge. Resistance fighters could be heard from each side of the Thames with their steps marching louder towards us. Chris passes me the cordon to the clock. I check in with Gerrard and Patience:

"Guys, are we ready?"

"We are, white boy. One second though,"

I wait for a brief moment only to hear a "Meow. Bitch. Meow" on the radio.

"Do us proud, Dom."

Once I struck that clock and the live stream was showing it, about one million people were to assault various guarded points across London, with the largest number, about 200,000, around Westminster. We have weakened their position but have not eliminated them yet. This is the final step and everyone knows it.

"To all of you watching this, London does not give up. London does not surrender. We stand together, we fall together, we rise together."

I look at Chris, who gives me the thumbs up. Our stream is followed by ten million people now. Explosions have started to be heard up and down the capital. Mrs Patel is ready to assault the Houses of Parliament alongside thousands of others. I look at the camera and raise my flag.

"For King and Adele... Onwards!"

Jets fly by, and this time they are ours. The gates of the Houses of Parliament are brought down and people swarm in. Sirens can be heard everywhere. It's chaos – but this time we know who's behind it. It's us.

To be continued…

WHAT TO EAT DURING THE APOCALYPSE

DOMINIC HARGRAVES

SPAGHETTI ALLA CARBONARA

(Alla Dom)

Serves 4

Ingredients:

350g spaghetti

150g pancetta or guanciale, diced (or lardons, if before pay day)

3 large eggs, plus 1 yolk

50g pecorino romano cheese, grated (accept no substitutes, this stuff's the real deal)

50g parmigiano reggiano

A generous pinch of freshly ground black pepper (because life's too short for bland food)

Method:

Start by bringing a large pot of salted water to a rolling boil. Once it's bubbling, toss in your spaghetti and cook it until it's *al dente*—firm to the bite, like a good comeback.

While your pasta works its carb-filled magic, heat a drizzle of olive oil in a skillet over medium heat. Add your choice of pork meat and let it sizzle away until it's golden and crispy. In a separate bowl, crack your eggs and add that extra yolk for good measure. Whisk them together adding equal parts Pecorino, Parmigiano, and a dash (or two) of pepper.

Once your pasta is cooked to perfection, drain it, reserving a cup of that starchy cooking water, and toss it back into the pot. Add your crispy pork bit, along with any leftover grease. Pour the cheesy-eggy mixture in and toss, adding the starchy water as necessary for your preferred consistency.

Serve and enjoy with another dash of pepper and Pecorino.

HAM AND CHEESE OMLETTE

Serves 1 Hungry Soul

Ingredients:

3 eggs

2 slices of ham, chopped (or ravished with your fingers!)

Handful of grated cheese

1 tbsp butter

Method:

Crack the eggs into a bowl and whisk until smooth.

Heat a frying pan over medium-high heat and add the butter.

Once the butter is melted and sizzling, pour in the whisked eggs. Allow the eggs to spread out in the pan and get to meet each other.

Sprinkle the ripped ham over one-half of the omelette. Top with grated cheese.

Fold the other half of the omelette over the filling.

Cook for 1-2 minutes until the cheese is melted and the omelette is golden.

Slide onto a plate and serve hot.

BACALAO A LAGAREIRO

Serves 2

Ingredients:

500g cod filet (bacalao), drained

4 large potatoes, peeled and cut into chunks

4 cloves of garlic, thinly sliced

1 onion, thinly sliced

1/2 cup olive oil

1 tbsp dried basil

Salt and pepper to taste

Fresh parsley for garnish

Method:

Preheat your oven to 200°C (400°F if you're American).

Place the drained cod fillet in a baking dish.

Arrange the potato chunks around the cod.

Heat the oil in a saucepan and cook the onion and garlic. (add dried basil if you wish!). Add to the baking dish.

Season with salt and pepper to taste.

Bake in the preheated oven for 25-30 minutes, or until the potatoes are tender and the fish is cooked through.

Garnish with fresh parsley before serving.

EGGS FLORENTINE

Serves 2

Ingredients:

4 large eggs

2 lovely English muffins, split and toasted

2 cups fresh spinach leaves

2 tbsp butter

2 tbsp plain flour

1 cup milk

Salt, pepper, nutmeg to taste

1/2 cup grated parmigiano

Method:

Melt butter, stir in flour, cook until golden. Gradually whisk in milk until smooth. Season with salt, pepper, and nutmeg. Stir in Parmigiano until melted then set aside.

Wilt spinach in a pan, and drain excess liquid. Spinach goes wrong fast, especially in an apocalypse, so always make good use of it.

Poach eggs until whites are set and place toasted muffins on plates then top with spinach. Add poached eggs on top of spinach and spoon warm cheese sauce over eggs.

BANGERS AND BEANS

Serves 3-4

Ingredients:

8 pork sausages (or veggie, save the world if you wish to eat mush!)

1 onion, chopped

2 cloves garlic, minced

2 cans cannellini beans, drained and rinsed

1 can diced tomatoes

1 cup chicken/veg broth

1 tbsp olive oil

1 tsp dried thyme

Salt and pepper to taste

Method:

Heat olive oil in a large skillet over medium heat. Add sausages and cook until browned on all sides. Remove from skillet and set aside.

In the same skillet, add onion and garlic. Sauté until softened. Stir in diced tomatoes and chicken/veg broth. Bring to a simmer. Add cannellini beans and dried thyme. Return sausages to the skillet, nestling them into the bean mixture.

Cover and simmer for 15-20 minutes, or until sausages are cooked through and flavours are and enjoy melded. Serve!

CHICKEN SOUP

Serves 4

Ingredients:

3-4 chicken legs

2 carrots, chopped

2 celery stalks, chopped

1 onion, diced

2 cloves garlic, minced

1.5 litres chicken broth

1 bay leaf

Method:

Start by preparing your vegetables: chop carrots, celery, onion, and mince garlic.

In a large pot, pour in the chicken broth and add the chopped vegetables. Place the whole chicken into the pot, ensuring it's fully submerged in the broth. Drop in a bay leaf for added flavour. Bring the pot to a gentle simmer over medium heat, then reduce the heat and let it simmer for about an hour, allowing all the flavours to meld together.

After 30 minutes, carefully remove the chicken from the pot and set it aside to rest. While the chicken is cooling, shred the meat from the bones. Return the chicken to the pot, stirring it into the soup. Enjoy and get rid of all illnesses with it.

PRAWN AND MAYO SANDWICH

Serves 2

Ingredients:

1 cup cooked prawns, peeled and deveined

1/4 cup mayonnaise

1 tbsp lemon juice

1 tbsp soy sauce

1 tbsp mustard 50g chopped dill/coriander

Slices of bread

Method:

Start by preparing your prawns: ensure they're peeled and deveined, fry for a few minutes in oil, then chop them into bite-sized pieces.

In a mixing bowl, combine the chopped prawns with mayonnaise, soy sauce, mustard and lemon juice. Add the dill or coriander, ensuring it's well combined. If desired,

lightly toast the slices of bread and spread butter on them for added flavour.

Spoon the prawn and mayo mixture onto the bread slice, spreading it evenly. Add another slice on top. Enjoy.

COQ AU VIN

Serves 2-3

Ingredients:

4 chicken thighs, bone-in and skin-on

200g bacon, diced

1 onion, chopped

2 cloves garlic, minced

200g button mushrooms, sliced

2 carrots, peeled and diced

2 cups red wine

1 cup chicken broth

2 tbsp tomato paste

2 sprigs fresh thyme

2 tbsp butter

Salt and pepper to taste

Method:

Begin by seasoning the chicken thighs with salt and pepper.

In a large skillet or Dutch oven, cook the diced bacon over medium heat until crispy. Remove the bacon from the pan and set aside, leaving the rendered fat in the pan.

Add the seasoned chicken thighs to the pan and brown them on both sides, about 5 minutes per side. Once browned, remove the chicken from the pan and set aside. In the same pan, add the chopped onion, minced garlic, sliced mushrooms, and diced carrots. Cook until the vegetables are softened, about 5-7 minutes.

Return the cooked bacon to the pan and stir to combine with the vegetables.

Pour in the red wine, chicken broth, and tomato paste, stirring to combine. Add the fresh thyme sprigs and bring the mixture to a simmer.

Once simmering, return the browned chicken thighs to the pan, nestling them into the sauce.

Cover the pan with a lid and simmer gently for 30-40 minutes, or until the chicken is cooked through and tender.

Remove the lid and stir in the butter until melted, adjusting the seasoning with salt and pepper if needed.

SCANDINAVIAN MEATBALLS

Serves 4

Ingredients:

500g ground beef

250g ground pork

1 onion, finely chopped

2 cloves garlic, minced

1/2 cup breadcrumbs

1/4 cup milk

1 egg

1 tsp salt

1/2 tsp black pepper

1/4 tsp nutmeg

1/4 tsp allspice

2 tbsp butter

2 tbsp plain flour

2 cups beef broth

1/2 cup heavy cream

Salt and pepper to taste

Chopped fresh parsley for garnish

Method:

In a large mixing bowl, combine the ground beef, ground pork, chopped onion, minced garlic, breadcrumbs, milk, egg, salt, pepper, nutmeg, and allspice. Mix until well combined.

Roll the meat mixture into small balls, about 1 inch in diameter.

In a large skillet, melt the butter over medium heat. Add the meatballs to the skillet and cook until browned on all sides, about 8-10 minutes. Remove the meatballs from the skillet and set aside.

In the same skillet, sprinkle the flour over the remaining butter and drippings. Cook, stirring constantly, for 1-2 minutes to make a roux.

Gradually pour in the beef broth, stirring constantly to prevent lumps from forming. Bring the mixture to a simmer.

Return the meatballs to the skillet, reduce the heat to low, and cover. Let the meatballs simmer gently for 20-25 minutes, or until cooked through.

Stir in the heavy cream and simmer for an additional 5 minutes to thicken the sauce.

Season the sauce with salt and pepper to taste.

Serve the Scandinavian meatballs hot over creamy mashed potatoes, garnished with chopped fresh parsley for a pop of colour and flavour. Enjoy this comforting and hearty dish with lingonberry jam on the side for an authentic Scandinavian experience.

OKRA SOUP

BY PATIENCE

Serves 4

Ingredients:

500g okra, sliced

1 onion, chopped

2 tomatoes, chopped

2 cloves garlic, minced

1 red bell pepper, chopped

1 green bell pepper, chopped

2 cups vegetable or chicken broth

400g canned chopped tomatoes

250g smoked turkey or chicken, chopped

1 tsp ground crayfish

1 tsp ground cayenne pepper (optional)

Salt and pepper to taste

2 tbsp palm oil or vegetable oil

Fresh parsley or coriander for garnish

Method:

In a large pot, heat the palm oil over medium heat. Add the chopped onion and minced garlic, and sauté until softened and fragrant, about 3-4 minutes.

Add the chopped tomatoes, red and green bell peppers, and sliced okra to the pot. Cook, stirring occasionally, for 5-7 minutes until the vegetables are slightly softened.

Pour in the vegetable or chicken broth and canned chopped tomatoes. Stir in the chopped smoked turkey or chicken, ground crayfish, and ground cayenne pepper if using. Season with salt and pepper to taste.

Bring the soup to a gentle simmer, then reduce the heat to low. Cover the pot and let the soup simmer for about 20-25 minutes, stirring occasionally, until the flavours meld together and the okra is tender.

Taste the soup and adjust the seasoning if needed.

Serve the okra soup hot, garnished with fresh parsley or coriander for a burst of freshness and colour.

BYRIANI

BY MR PATEL (HERO)

Serves 4

Ingredients:

500g boneless chicken, cut into bite-sized pieces

2 cups basmati rice, washed and soaked for 30 minutes in cold water

1 large onion, thinly sliced

2 tomatoes, chopped

1/2 cup plain yogurt

2 tbsp ginger-garlic paste

1 tbsp biryani masala powder

1 tsp ground turmeric

1 tsp ground cumin

1 tsp ground coriander

1 tsp red chilli powder

4 cups chicken broth

1/4 cup chopped fresh coriander

1/4 cup chopped fresh mint leaves

2 tablespoons ghee or vegetable oil

Salt to taste

Method:

In a large bowl, marinate the chicken pieces with yoghurt, ginger-garlic paste, biryani masala powder, turmeric, cumin, coriander, red chilli powder, and salt. Let it marinate for at least 30 minutes or overnight in the refrigerator for more flavour.

Heat the ghee or vegetable oil in a large pot over medium heat. Add the thinly sliced onion and sauté until golden brown and caramelized about 10-12 minutes.

Add the marinated chicken pieces to the pot and cook until they are browned on all sides, about 5-7 minutes.

Stir in the chopped tomatoes and cook until they soften and release their juices, about 5 minutes.

Drain the soaked rice and add it to the pot. Gently stir to combine with the chicken and tomato mixture.

Pour in the chicken broth and bring the mixture to a boil. Once boiling, reduce the heat to low, cover the pot with a tight-fitting lid, and let the biryani simmer for about 20-25 minutes until the rice is cooked through and the chicken is tender.

Remove the pot from the heat and let it sit, covered, for an additional 5-10 minutes to allow the flavours to infuse the dish.

Fluff the biryani with a fork and garnish with chopped fresh coriander and mint leaves before serving.

BHAJIS

BY MRS PATEL

Serves 4

Ingredients:

2 large onions, thinly sliced

1 cup chickpea flour (besan)

2 tbsp rice flour

1 tsp ground cumin

1 tsp ground coriander

1/2 tsp turmeric powder

1/2 tsp chilli powder (adjust to taste)

1/2 tsp baking soda

1/2 cup chopped fresh coriander

Salt to taste

Water, as needed

Vegetable oil for frying

Method:

In a large mixing bowl, combine the chickpea flour, rice flour, ground cumin, ground coriander, turmeric powder, chilli powder, baking soda, chopped cilantro, and salt. Mix well to combine.

Add water gradually to the dry ingredients, whisking continuously, until you have a thick batter consistency. The batter should be thick enough to coat the back of a spoon.

Add the thinly sliced onions to the batter and mix until they are well coated.

In a deep frying pan, heat vegetable oil over medium heat until hot but not smoking.

Take a small portion of the onion and batter mixture using your fingers or a spoon and carefully drop it into the hot oil. Repeat this process, frying a few bhajis at a time, making sure not to overcrowd the pan.

Fry the onion bhajis for 3-4 minutes on each side, or until they are golden brown and crispy.

WHAT TO KEEP AROUND IN CASE OF AN APOCALYPSE

A work-in-progress list by Chris and Dom

- *Tinned Tuna (or other meats!)*
- *Sweetcorn*
- *Beans*
- *Canned fruits*
- *Pasta and rice*
- *Nuts*
- *Oils*
- *Flour*
- *Coffee, Tea – in case you need to be awake*
- *Biscuits*

CHRIS' BURGERS

Serves 4

Ingredients:

500g minced beef

Salt and pepper to taste

4 hamburger buns

Optional toppings: lettuce, tomato, onion, cheese, pickles, ketchup, mustard, mayonnaise

Method:

Preheat your skillet over medium-high heat. Divide the ground beef into four equal portions and shape each portion into a patty, about 1/2 to 3/4 inch thick. Season both sides of the patties generously with salt and pepper. Add a bit of oil to the pan.

Cook the patties for about 4-5 minutes per side, or until they reach your desired level of doneness. Avoid pressing down on the patties with a spatula while cooking, as this can cause them to lose moisture.

While the patties are cooking, toast the hamburger buns on the grill or in a toaster until lightly golden.

Once the patties are cooked, remove them from the grill or skillet and let them rest for a few minutes.

Assemble your burgers by placing each patty on a toasted bun and adding your desired toppings.

MUSHROOM RISOTTO

WITH HELP FROM GERRARD

Serves 4

Ingredients:

1 cup arborio rice

2 cups vegetable broth

1 cup dried mushrooms (such as porcini or shiitake)

1/2 cup white wine (optional)

1 small onion, finely chopped

2 cloves garlic, minced

2 tbsp olive oil

1/4 cup grated parmigiano cheese

Salt and pepper to taste

Method:

Place the dried mushrooms in a bowl and cover them with hot water. Let them soak for about 20-30 minutes, or until they are rehydrated and soft. Once rehydrated, drain the mushrooms, reserving the soaking liquid, and chop them into smaller pieces if necessary.

In a saucepan, heat the vegetable broth over low heat until warm. Keep it warm on the stove while you prepare the risotto.

In a large skillet (or makeshift underground sign plate), heat the olive oil over medium heat. Add the chopped onion and minced garlic, and sauté until softened and translucent, about 2-3 minutes.

Add the Arborio rice to the skillet and stir to coat it with the oil, onions, and garlic. Cook for another 1-2 minutes, stirring frequently, until the rice is lightly toasted.

Pour in the white wine (if using) and cook, stirring constantly, until the liquid has been absorbed by the rice.

Begin adding the warm vegetable broth to the rice, one ladleful at a time, stirring constantly and allowing each addition of broth to be absorbed before adding more. Continue this process until the rice is creamy and tender, but still slightly al dente, about 20-25 minutes.

About halfway through the cooking process, add the chopped rehydrated mushrooms to the risotto, along with a splash of the reserved mushroom soaking liquid, for extra flavour.

Once the rice is cooked to your desired consistency, remove the skillet from the heat and stir in the grated parmigiano cheese.

BACK TO ORIGINS

Like every other self-respecting immigrant on these shores, I take pride in my upbringing and the challenges and development it brought. It would be disrespectful of me to have written a first book and not have a sprinkle of Romanian in it. If you've made it this far, let me share just a couple of things and a few more recipes with you.

Whilst my dad was a heavy influence on channelling my inner writer, my mother shared her passion and love for cooking with me. Like millions of mothers out there, she always made time to cook a meal with heart, only for my sister and I to get fussy and never be pleased at the same time.

When I first arrived for university in the UK I was your average student, eating ready-made meals and the occasional pan-fried meat. My mother, seeing my desolate state of being, took me under her wings in a bootcamp-style introduction to cooking. Whilst apprehensive at first, my pursuits for physical love have made me improve the other love languages I was speaking. Realising that I might need to supplement my personality at times, I discovered great pleasure in communicating my love to others through cooking. The simple became more complicated and now I love a challenge, despite my amateur style of cooking.

I could talk about Romania being the greatest place on earth and other such immigrant tropes, but I'm not going to do that. I think people make places more than borders and my people love food. So, if there's one way I can share a bit of my heritage with others, with the help of this book, it is by including some of my mom's recipes at the end. Apart from the dessert, for obvious reasons, I tried to keep it with a good amount of similar ingredients: *cabbage* and *minced meat*. They are used extensively in Romanian cooking and a lot of our home cooking is done trying to minimise waste and make more out of less. Have a go!

Pofta buna! – the Romanian Bon Appetit!

CIORBA DE PERISOARE

MEATBALL SOUR SOUP

A staple of Romanian cuisine and one not missing from must lunches – ciorba is a sour soup that has many varieties. As a kid, I was forced to sit down and finish my ciorba before I could go for the mains. I used to hate it and now there's no week going by wishing I had a sour soup to start the feast with.

Serves 4

Ingredients:

3-400g pork mince (beef or mix okay too)

1 or 2 eggs

50g of rice or a slice of bread (for meatball mixture)

1 onion, sliced and diced

50g of parsley, thinly chopped

1 carrot

1 small celery root

2 litres bone broth (pork or beef) – or simply water!

500ml sour cabbage brine or borsch/ lemon juice

1 tbsp of plain flour

Method:

Meatballs

In a bowl, mix the minced meat with the rice, half the parsley, egg and onion and add salt and pepper.

Form tiny meatballs and roll them in flour, letting them rest on a plate.

Ciorba

Separately, in a large pot, lightly fry the rest of the vegetables in a bit of oil, until they soften.

Add the bone broth (or water) and let it simmer for half an hour on medium-low heat for the vegetables to cook. Boil the sour cabbage juice (lemon/or borsch) in another pot and after it boils, add it to the bone broth. If you have spare bits of sour cabbage add them in too.

Add the meatballs one by one and wait about 10 minutes for them to cook, they will rise to the top. Make sure you're keeping the pot on medium-low.

Turn the hob off, add the remaining parsley leaves and let it rest for another 10 minutes.

Enjoy with a tablespoon of sour cream added at the end or some chillies.

SARMALE

– ROLLS OF MINCED MEAT, WRAPPED IN CABBAGE LEAVES.

Another classic, shared by many Balkan or Arab countries – you will be offered this in most places at most times, but particularly popular around Christmas.

Serves 6

Ingredients:

700g of mixed minced meat (pork and beef/ lamb and beef)

1 medium onion

100g of rice

3 tbsp of tomato paste

50g of fresh dill

1 tbsp of dried thyme

2 sour cabbages (in brine)

1 tbsp sweet paprika

2 tsp vegetable oil

Method:

Step 1 – Preparing the cabbage

Separate the leaves individually and wash them. Cut any stalks and place them on top of eachother on a plate. Depending on the size of the sarmale you may want to cut the leaves in halves or thirds.

Step 2 – Preparing the mix

Wash the rice and let it soak in some cold water for a few minutes. Slice and dice the onion and fry it lightly in a pan. After a minute add the rice to fry too, mixing gently. Sprinkle some sweet paprika and add a cup of water letting the rice and veggies boil until the rice is done. Let it cool down and add the mince meat with the rice in a bowl and mix well, adding salt pepper and thyme.

Step 3 – Rolling it

Have a piece of cabbage stretched in your palm and add one tablespoon of mixture in the middle. Roll the leaf to cover the mixture and make sure to tighten the ends. They will expand when cooking.

Step 4 – Boiling it

In a dutch oven or casserole dish, add two tablespoons of oil, and place some leftover sliced cabbage leaves at the bottom. Place the rolled sarmale one by one trying to not leave space in between them. Feel free to add more salt, pepper and thyme over the first layer. Repeat until you run out of sarmale. At the top add some more sliced cabbage leaves. If cooking in the oven, leave on 180 degrees for 2-3 hours – pouring tomato paste over halfway through. On the hob, cook for half the time on medium heat.

PAPANASI

– FRIED CHEESE DOUGHNUTS

In my lifetime of sharing Romanian food with others, these were always a winner. A sweet treat at the end of the meal, these little doughs of joy take me back down memory lane always.

Serves 6

Ingredients:

500g cottage cheese

2 eggs

A few drops of rum essence/aroma

75g granulated sugar

1 sachet vanilla sugar

230-250g plain flour

1 tsp baking soda

Vegetable oil for frying the doughnuts

250g smetana or crème fraiche to serve

Whole fruit runny blueberry jam to serve or sour cherry, blackberry, black currant jam etc

Method:

Place the drained cottage cheese into a bowl. Add the eggs and the rum aroma, the granulated and vanilla sugar. With an immersion blender, blend the ingredients until you obtain a rough paste.

Mix about 230g of the flour and the baking soda and add them to the cheese mixture. Mix with a spoon. Flour the working surface and your hands generously and knead to form a ball. The dough should still be somewhat sticky yet manageable.

Divide the dough into 9 balls. Roll 8 of the balls into thick sausages and unite the sausage ends to get a circle with a hole in the middle. Use the last ball to make 8 little balls, which will be used to top the *papanasi*.

In the meantime, heat the oil in a pot. Use enough oil to cover the dough balls.

Add a few *papanasi* and do not overcrowd the pan; they should be able to move around freely.

Turn the heat down to medium-low. Turn the doughnuts with a slotted spoon a few times in between and fry until they are golden brown. This should take anything between 5-10 minutes

Place them on plates lined with kitchen paper and dry them to absorb some excess fat.

Serve warm topped with smetana (or crème fraiche) and blueberry jam. Place the little balls on top and top them with a bit of smetana and jam as well.

ACKNOWLEDGEMENTS

Whilst I did write this by myself, the people who have shaped and supported me on this journey should not go unnoticed to avoid awkward chats after publication. For without their help, this book would've just become an obsolete file in a folder that contains memes, job applications and questionable downloaded songs (legally, your honour).

I'd like to start by thanking my partner, Bushra, foremost. Your unconditional love has gotten me through the darkest of times and your unshaken belief in me was energy for the months before. I wouldn't have done it without you, and I'm grateful beyond words for your existence. I wish for everyone to feel as safe and supported by someone as I've felt by you. I love you.

To my mother, Alina, and my father, Laurentiu – thank you for being my raunchiest supporters and my harshest critics, and the ones never stopping me from pushing for my potential, encouraging me with love all the way. Whatever idea I've had, you've supported, even at times through gritted teeth. To my younger sister, Raluca, thanks for being a close friend more than anything. I've said it before, and I'll put it here for posterity – I'm proud of the principled, strong woman you have become.

To my teachers, in particular Mrs Nedelcu, my "second" mom, thank you for believing in me when my life could've taken other turns. We may not always have agreed on everything, but your love and support have uplifted and formed me.

My friends, too many to name, we may not speak as often, we may not see each other as much as we'd wish, such is life... I carry you with me on all my journeys and I know you're watching. I don't believe in spiritual stuff, but I'm always there for you and I always feel you supporting and rooting for me.

To my beta readers and all the people who have helped me bring this book to life, thank you for the kind words, the constructive criticism, and the honest encouragement. You made me believe in this book and made me push it to the point that this person holding it right now, knows of your existence.

And ultimately, but equally important – you, the reader. Whoever you are, for whatever reason you have picked me, for whatever discounted price you bought my book. An author is just a writer without an audience and with a large expense bill without you. I'd like to think that if you've made it this far you enjoyed it! Thank you, from the bottom of my heart.

*Make sure to let me know your thoughts! On www.vladimir-stefan.co.uk and socials @vladimirstefan_*

Milton Keynes UK
Ingram Content Group UK Ltd.
UKHW010653240624
444429UK00003B/19